He looked at her, and she knew. He was going to kiss her.

He tipped her head back with one finger and brought his mouth to hers. The instant their lips touched, the kiss spun into a roller-coaster ride of sensation.

She'd expected his kiss to be polished and calculated, a process to get from point A to point C. There was no point A. There was only a mating of lips and air and instinct.

When it was over, she held perfectly still. Her breath seemed to have solidified in her throat. She hadn't been kissed in a long time. And never quite like this.

"I shouldn't have come here."

"I disagree."

"I should go home."

"It's only five days, Madeline. If you leave, you'll never know what would have happened during those five days."

She wondered how it would feel to be so sure of something. She used to be that sure. That felt like another woman's life.

Dear Reader,

Writing this letter to you started me thinking about letters—letters, not e-mails or text messages. Letters like those our grandmothers wrote to our grandpas, mothers to daughters, and old college roommates to each other. They were lyrical and poignant, awaited, savored and treasured.

They were gifts from one heart to another. My newest book, *The Wedding Gift,* has something in common with those old-fashioned letters, for this story is a gift from my heart to yours.

I'm so pleased to be part of Silhouette's lineup of wedding stories this month, for our youngest and oldest sons were married recently, nine months apart. All four of our sons are married now, and each wedding is a poignant memory and each daughter-in-law a wonderful addition to our family. The babies are arriving, too—oh my, what blessings they are! I promise I won't bring out their pictures, but don't be surprised when babies are featured in my upcoming books.

But first things first: I hope you enjoy, no, I hope you savor *The Wedding Gift.* May reading it speak to your heart the way writing it spoke to mine.

Until next time and always,

Sandra

THE WEDDING GIFT

SANDRA STEFFEN

SPECIAL EDITION®

Published by Silhouette Books

America's Publisher of Contemporary Romance

 SILHOUETTE BOOKS

Recycling programs
for this product may
not exist in your area.

ISBN-13: 978-0-373-65532-8

THE WEDDING GIFT

SANDRA STEFFEN

has always been a storyteller. She began nurturing this hidden talent by concocting adventures for her brothers and sisters, even though the boys were more interested in her ability to hit a baseball over the barn—an automatic homerun. She didn't begin her pursuit of publication until she was a young wife and mother of four sons. Since her thrilling debut as a published author in 1992, more than thirty-five of her novels have graced bookshelves across the country.

This winner of a RITA® Award, a Wish Award and a National Readers' Choice Award enjoys traveling with her husband. Usually their destinations are settings for her upcoming books. They are empty nesters these days. Who knew it could be so much fun? Please visit her at www.sandrasteffen.com.

For the newlyweds
Greg and Maggie
and
Mike and Amber

Acknowledgment

A special thanks to Barb DePue for sharing incredibly
detailed information and unforgettable descriptions of
her husband Bruce's heart transplant. The Internet is nice,
but there's nothing like a long talk with an old friend.

Chapter One

Madeline Sullivan tiptoed from her attic apartment by the light of the waning moon. She crept down two flights of stairs and across floorboards so old they normally creaked beneath the weight of dust bunnies, yet she didn't awaken any of the inn's guests. Her car started on the first try and she didn't see another pair of headlights until she'd reached the first orchard west of town. From there she drove north to the river, then west and north again all the way to Lake Michigan.

The weather cooperated and the traffic was manageable. Even the faded no-trespassing sign marking the narrow lane she was searching for practically jumped out at her at first glance.

It was almost too easy.

Easy was fine. Easy was wonderful. Really.

She didn't need the accompaniment of distant thunder or the reassurance of rainbows. What she needed was waiting at the top of a knoll near the Sleeping Bear Dunes National Lakeshore.

At least she hoped it was.

Her heart *did* race as she turned onto the lane, but that was just her better judgment rearing its timid little head. Determinedly gripping the steering wheel with both hands, she followed the winding path to the top of the hill overlooking the enormous sand dunes for which the shore had been named. Beyond the dunes the choppy waters of Lake Michigan disappeared into a solid wall of clouds. The sky had been low and gray all week, a welcome sight in the scorching heat of summer, but on this day in early spring, the clouds were an annoying affront to the promise of fair weather.

Madeline wasn't looking for promises. She was looking for a man named Riley Merrick.

Rolling to a stop where dune grass still brittle from the harsh winter concealed most of her car, she settled back to wait. If her sources were accurate, Merrick was the architect overseeing the construction of an extravagant vacation home a quarter mile away.

There was no sign of him, though. She watched for several minutes before reaching for her cell phone to let her best friend back home know she'd arrived safely.

As usual, Summer Matthews started talking the moment she put her phone to her ear. "Since this isn't a collect call, I assume you haven't been arrested for stalking Riley Merrick. Yet."

"Most people begin conversations with hello, Summer. Besides, I'm not stalking him."

"I suppose you're not peering through binoculars right now, either."

Being careful not to let the binoculars clank against her cell phone, Madeline hummed something noncommittal. She was a terrible liar, but even if she'd been good at it, she wouldn't have lied to Summer.

"If you'd called five minutes sooner," Summer said, "your brothers could have participated in the conversation."

Summer was the owner of the Old Stone Inn in Orchard Hill. Once a stop on a well-traveled stage line, the old building was now a popular bed-and-breakfast inn. It sat on a hill overlooking the small city of Orchard Hill to the east and the river and the surrounding apple orchards to the north and west. The resident innkeeper, Summer was known to everyone back home as the keeper of secrets. She was also the best friend Madeline had ever had.

"The boys came to the inn?" Madeline asked.

"After lunch. All three of them. All at once," Summer said drolly.

Oh, dear. All three Sullivan men all at once intimidated most people. Madeline's conscience chafed. She wished she could have done this without sneaking, but if her brothers had known she was planning this today, they would have tried to stop her, or worse, insisted upon coming with her. God love them, but they would smother her if she let them.

"What did you tell them?" she asked.

"First I reminded them that you're a grown woman. Marsh took it the hardest. You should have seen the look on his face when I broke the news that you're twenty-five. I informed Reed that seeking proof that Riley Merrick is alive and well isn't unreasonable and I made Noah promise not to follow you by land, by sky or by sea. I didn't have the heart to tell any of them I advised you to have your way with the first gorgeous man you laid eyes on."

It was such ludicrous advice Madeline couldn't help smiling. "I'm overlooking a construction site, Summer. Think about what you're suggesting."

Of everyone Madeline loved, Summer understood her best. She would have gladly helped Madeline find a way to shed her old life, to sprout wings or start over where no one knew her, the way Summer had. But she wasn't like Summer. Marsh, Reed and Noah had done nothing wrong except love their younger sister, and perhaps try too hard to fill their parents' shoes after they died when she was twelve.

Madeline knew how worried everyone was about her, but her friends, family and coworkers couldn't fix what was wrong with her life. The only person who could make things better was Madeline herself.

And maybe Riley Merrick.

"Have you seen him yet?"

Summer's voice summoned Madeline back to the situation at hand. Studying the view through the field glasses again, she said, "There've been a few vehicles in and out of the gate and a small crew is climbing around on some scaffolding right now. I don't think he's with them."

"He's probably short, fat and bald, you know."

"He isn't short, fat or bald," Madeline said absently as she searched the faces of two new arrivals in the distance.

"How do you know?" Summer asked.

"I Googled him."

There was a moment of silence before Summer said, "So what does he look like?"

"Early thirties, with dark, unruly hair, deep-set

eyes, a stubborn chin and a stance that has attitude written all over it."

"He sounds dreamy."

"Don't start, Summer. I mean it."

"I'm just having a little fun. It's been a long time since you've had any fun. Maybe it's been long enough."

Summer had spoken gently, the way everyone in Madeline's life did these days, and yet the words found their way into her chest like an echo returning from a distant canyon.

"What will you do after you've seen him?" Summer asked. "Will you try to talk to him?"

"I don't think so. I mean, what would I say? 'Excuse me. You don't know me, but I just drove a hundred and eighty miles because I need to believe in the notion that something good can come from even the saddest tragedies. You see, that heart beating in your chest used to be my late fiancé's.' Can you imagine how it would feel to hear *that* out of the blue? I didn't come here to upset him."

"I know," Summer said. "It isn't asking too much though, to know he's alive and flourishing."

"Thanks, Summer. You're the best."

Madeline stared into the clouds in the distance for a long time after the call ended, her mind blessedly blank. Eventually the low rumble of an approaching car brought her from her trance. After raising the binoculars to her eyes, she saw a silver Porsche pull into the lane leading to the construction site. The driver parked on the crest of the next hill and got out. Wearing a brown bomber jacket and khakis, he turned, giving her a momentary glimpse of dark, unruly hair and deep-set eyes.

Riley Merrick. His name escaped on a whisper and brought with it a hitch in her breathing.

He left his car well away from the bulldozer lumbering back and forth at the foot of the hill, and walked the rest of the way to the site. He moved like a long-distance runner, strong and focused and seemingly oblivious to the cold wind in his face.

With his arrival, the area came alive. Generators were started and men in tool belts climbed up scaffolding and ladders, spreading out at the top like ants at a picnic.

Madeline settled back in her seat and took a deep breath. There. She'd done it. She'd witnessed for herself that Riley was alive, and yes, apparently flourishing. Now she could spend the rest of her vacation anywhere, satisfied in her newfound knowledge.

There was only one tiny little problem with that. She didn't feel satisfied. She felt—

She jerked her head around and fumbled for the

binoculars. Someone was climbing the scaffolding in the distance, someone as lithe and agile as a long-distance runner, someone wearing a brown bomber and khakis.

The field glasses bounced off the passenger seat and thudded to the floor. Seconds later she was starting her car. Tires churning up sand, she raced down the hill, around the bend and through the gates at the construction site. In an instant she was out of the car, running against the wind.

The blueprints in Riley's hands flapped in the wind as he watched the crane lift a roof truss high over the heads of the crew bracing to secure it into place. This summer house was going to be a beauty. From its conception he'd envisioned a buxom lady, with her turret windows, soaring vaulted ceilings and pitched roof. The clients, an eccentric movie-producing husband-and-wife duo from L.A. wanted a showplace, and Riley was just the architect to ensure they got exactly what they wanted.

The lakeside lady would boast stone quarried in Michigan's upper peninsula and incredible arched leaded windows that winked in just the right light. Inside, she'd have every decadent luxury—a gourmet kitchen, heated stone and Brazilian cherry floors, steam showers and a spa fit for royalty. She'd be a big-boned gal, six thousand square feet on one floor with another fourteen hundred in the nearby guesthouse. By the average person's standards, that was a lot of square footage for a vacation home. It seemed the wealthier people were, the more room they needed to get away from each other. Riley grew up in a house twice this size.

From the corner of his eye, he saw his project foreman sauntering toward him. "Phone's for you," Kipp Dawson said.

"The clients?" Riley asked. When Kipp shook his head, Riley tensed, for only his mother could elicit a grimace of this magnitude from a man as tough and rangy as Kipp. "Take a message," he said through gritted teeth.

"Do I look like a secretary to you?" But Kipp punched a button on his phone and said, "He'll call you later, Chloe," then promptly broke the connection.

Upon meeting them, people were often surprised by Kipp and Riley's friendship, for Riley had had a privileged upbringing and Kipp had been left with any relative not quick enough to barricade the door. When Kipp was fourteen his mother had dropped him at the Merrick estate, claiming Riley's father was Kipp's old man, too. Since Jay Merrick had been good at two things—making money and siring sons, it was certainly possible. In those days before DNA testing, it had taken private investigators nearly a year to prove it wasn't true. By then the boys were close and Riley's mother told Kipp he was welcome to stay. She never let either of them forget her good deed.

Riley knew his mother was worried about him but he didn't appreciate her meddling. Kipp tolerated it much better. Of course, he had her up on a pedestal, right where she wanted to be. "Sooner or later you're going to have to talk to her," he said.

Riley mumbled something that meant the subject was closed, but the truth was, he knew what his mother wanted. He'd been dodging her calls all week.

He and Kipp stood side by side while the crew struggled to heave the next truss into place. At this rate they'd never get them all secured before that storm blew ashore.

"Where is everyone?" Riley asked.

"Billie's sick, Art's still out with that bum knee of his and the Trevino brothers didn't show up again," Kipp said as he lit a cigarette.

"Feel like making yourself useful?" Riley asked.

Kipp hadn't leaned on a razor in a while. The whisker stubble didn't conceal his eagerness as he ground the cigarette into the sand. "Your mother's gonna have my boys in a sling. I'm right behind you."

They donned safety vests and climbed up. The moment Riley took his place with the crew, an age-old thrill went through him, the kind of thrill that inspired men to shout from distant mountaintops, to dance around ceremonial campfires and to raise a flag on the moon.

The view was breathtaking in every direction. A car was speeding down one of the narrow lanes wending through the nearby hills. Out on the lake an iron ore tanker plodded due south. A small barge chugged away from it, giving it a wide berth. In the distance the sun turned the clouds into a sieve, sprinkling light like holy water across the surface of Lake Michigan.

Riley had climbed mountains and skied down them, flown airplanes and parachuted out of them. Speed was good. High altitudes were better. It wasn't that the world made sense off the ground. Off the ground, it didn't have to make sense. Up here, it didn't matter that he'd contracted a rare virus that should have killed him and would have if not for modern medicine. Up here he didn't feel as if he'd been walking in another man's shoes for the past eighteen months.

Every man in the crew watched the crane lift the next truss into the air. Everyone braced as it was lowered toward them. Every one of them saw it lurch on a sudden gust of wind then slam into Riley's chest.

Riley felt the impact, heard the rush of air leaving his lungs. He fell twenty feet in an instant and snapped to the end of the cable attached to his safety vest with a force that knocked the remaining wind out of him.

"Pete, Sean!" the foreman yelled. "Get that rafter nailed down. Hold on, boss!"

Cinched tight in his harness twenty feet off the ground, Riley wasn't going anywhere. He was aware of more discussion overhead, but the next voice he concentrated on came from halfway down the wall.

"Riley. Over here."

Kipp was perched at the edge of the scaffolding. His left arm was wrapped around a two-by-eight runner as he tossed Riley a rope and drew him to solid footing. Once safely on the scaffolding, Riley unhooked his harness and released it. He had little choice but to withstand the quick once-over Kipp gave him with a gaze that saw everything. The fact that he didn't shrug it off and go back to work wasn't lost on anybody, least of all on Riley himself. Shakier than he cared to admit, he carefully climbed the rest of the way to the ground.

And came face-to-face with a woman he didn't know.

Or was he seeing things? After all, pretty young women didn't appear out of nowhere at rough-in sites. This one seemed to be floating toward him. Her hair was long and light blond. Her lips were moving but it was difficult to understand what she was saying.

"Are you all right? Are you feeling faint? Can you hear me? How many fingers am I holding up?"

Riley stared dazedly at her. She was of average height and wore a light jacket that was belted at her waist and open at her throat where a silver charm hung from a delicate chain. Her breathing was shallow and her eyes flashed with the same beams of light that surrounded the rest of her.

Beams of light? What the hell was wrong with him?

He scrubbed a hand over his face to clear his vision. Thankfully when he looked again, the strange light was gone. The woman hadn't disappeared, though.

"You're sweating," she said. "You could be going into shock. You should be sitting down. Lying down would be better. How are your ribs? Are they tender? Do you have pain anywhere? There's no telling what you might have bruised or injured or God forbid, jarred loose."

She opened an oversized purse and fished around inside. The next thing he knew, she was trying to press the end of a stethoscope to his chest.

He backed out of her reach.

"I'm a nurse," she said gently. "Don't worry, I've done this a thousand times."

He closed his hand around the end of the stetho-scope and held it away from his body. She tried again to push it toward his chest but he held fast. Before either of them was ready to admit they'd reached an impasse, the wind intervened, dragging her hair out of the fastener at her nape, an effective diversion for both of them. Free, the blond tresses whipped and swirled around her head.

She finally released her end of the stethoscope and reached up, winsomely tying her hair into a knot that begged to be undone again. She should have looked as out of place as an orchid in a patch of quack grass, and yet her presence seemed expected, binding somehow.

Awareness surged through him so strongly he was tempted to forget he was standing in the middle of a construction site in plain view of a dozen curious men with a pretty young woman intent upon touch-ing him. He wanted her to touch him almost as much as he wanted to pull her to him and cover her mouth with his.

"I'd feel a lot better if you would sit down," she said. "Could I at least take your pulse?"

The question finally brought him to his senses. She was a nurse. Here to take his pulse.

The thundering in his ears moved ominously into his voice as he said, "My mother sent you, didn't she?"

Chapter Two

Riley Merrick was standing three feet away.

Madeline was certain her feet were planted firmly on the ground, and yet she felt as if she were drawing closer to him. Heat emanated from him, making her yearn to burrow into his warmth, her ear pressed to his chest. The rumble of the bulldozer's engine and the sharp pounding of heavy hammers receded until the only sound she heard was the chiming of something sweet and delicate sprinkling into the empty spaces inside her.

"Well? Did my mother hire you or didn't she?"

She blinked. And sound returned in a raucous,

roaring cacophony of pitch and volume. "Your mother?" she finally asked.

He scowled. "Knowing my mother, she probably told you to lie about your association with her."

"I'm a terrible liar," she said dazedly.

He finally released the stethoscope. "Keep that away from me. Who are you, anyway?"

"I'm Madeline Sullivan. As I told you before, I'm a nurse, but—"

"So my mother sent you to play nursemaid. That's so typical. No doubt she expects you to check my pulse and report back to her."

Since she still didn't know what his mother had to do with her, she said, "I think we should keep your mother out of this."

"At least we agree on one thing."

"Do we also agree that walking on narrow beams fifty feet off the ground is a risk you have no business taking?" Why was she so breathless?

Angry, he was having trouble breathing, too. His next attempt made his nostrils flare as he said, "I was wearing my safety harness."

Eyeing the harness dangling from the end of a yellow rope, his hard hat upside down on the plywood floor directly beneath it, she shook her head. He could have broken his neck. He could have *died,* and it all would have been for nothing.

"It can take a long time for ribs to heal completely after a surgery like yours," she said gently. "Especially with the medications you're on. You are taking your medicine, aren't you?"

His eyes narrowed and his voice lowered as he said, "You're fired, Madeline."

Her head jerked up. "You can't fire me."

"I just did."

She had to force her gaping mouth closed. Now that she wasn't simply absorbing the essence of him, she had the presence of mind to take a good look at the man whose name had crept into her thoughts so often these past eighteen months.

She'd expected his face to be swollen, his jowls sagging, his skin sallow. Instead he was lean and rugged and tan. A muscle moved in his jaw and there was a trace of something not easily identified in his brown eyes. Was it dread? Regret? Or was it a haunting sorrow?

Cursed with a soft spot for anyone suffering or struggling in any way, she laid a hand on his arm and said, "What you're feeling is perfectly natural."

He drew his arm out of her grasp. "You can't possibly know what I'm feeling. You have to leave. This is private property and you're trespassing. Tell my mother—never mind. I'll tell her myself." With that, he walked away.

She watched as he conferred with a burly man who'd just climbed off the earthmover. The other man glanced at her, putting her in mind of a St. Bernard—big, yes, hairy, certainly, loyal, obviously, but not very fierce. Deciding to spare *him* the discomfort of having to escort her to her car, and spare herself the discomfort, as well, she left of her own accord. She surprised herself when she slammed her foot on the accelerator, but she had to admit the sound of sand spraying behind her spinning tires brought her a certain satisfaction.

No sense letting Riley Merrick have the last word.

"Uh-huh," she said absently into the phone as she reached ahead to wipe fog off her windshield. The hills on either side of the county road were dotted with cherry trees, the branches flexed in anticipation of that elusive signal from Mother Nature to burst into blossom. Madeline understood their wistful impatience.

"Was Riley anything like you expected?" Summer asked.

Hunkering down in her seat, she wrapped her jacket more tightly around her to ward off the damp chill while she considered the question. There was a rawness about Riley Merrick, a burning sensuality that had caught her completely off guard. Deciding to keep that perception to herself for now, she said, "He's fit, healthy and stubborn, and he looks like his photo."

"Are you coming home now?" Summer asked.

Madeline had been sitting along the side of the road for the past forty minutes, thinking about her options. Glancing at the keys dangling uselessly in the ignition, she said, "That would be problematic."

"Why? What aren't you telling me?"

"What you don't know the boys can't badger out of you." She jolted when a knock sounded on the window. Clearing a spot on the foggy glass, she saw a woman in coveralls hunkered down, looking in.

"Did you just gasp?" Summer asked.

Madeline rubbed the tender spot on her forehead where she'd smacked it on the window and nodded at the woman who'd startled her. To Summer, she said, "How do you suppose a two-ton tow truck sneaked up on me?"

"You called a tow truck?" Summer asked.

Gesturing to the driver that she'd be with her in a moment, Madeline said, "My car started wheezing as I left the construction site. I managed to coax it a mile before it lunged to the side of the road and surrendered. It's what I get for having the last word."

"I'm not even going to try to make sense of that."

She could picture Summer pacing from the front

desk of the inn to the French doors with the view of the back garden, always on the lookout, for what Madeline didn't like to imagine. "They told me they were sending out someone named Red. I wasn't expecting a woman. I have to go."

"You'll call me if you need me?" Summer asked.

"You know I will." With that, she dropped her phone into her bag, unlocked her door and got out.

"Are you Madeline Sullivan?" the other woman asked.

Madeline nodded. "*You're* Red?"

"It's Ruby, actually. Red is my dad." She touched a ringlet that had escaped the confinement of her ball cap. "Runs in the family."

There was a feeling Madeline had when she was exactly where she was supposed to be at the precise moment she was supposed to be there. Some called it an "ah" moment. She called it *knowing*. She'd described it once to Summer as a shimmering energy that resembled light and felt like warmth. She'd experienced it the day Summer had driven into Orchard Hill six years ago, the day Aaron Andrews took the vacant desk next to her in the fifth grade, and fleetingly when she'd first encountered Riley Merrick today. It was happening again right now.

"Do I have grease on my face?" Ruby asked.

Madeline chided herself for staring. "Goodness,

no. I was just thinking how much your name suits you. You're gorgeous. How tall are you?"

"Five-eleven." Ruby opened the door and put the car in Neutral. "And a quarter," she added quietly.

Ruby may have been shy about her exotic beauty, but Madeline soon discovered she wasn't shy about anything else. She talked while she hooked the cable to the front axle, while she started the winch and while she pointed them toward town.

Listening, Madeline learned what it had been like growing up in Gale, a small town twenty miles west of Traverse City, and how Ruby had decided early on that the family business wasn't for her. Ruby had reached the point in her life story where she'd graduated from the University of Chicago when Madeline noticed the silver car in the side mirror.

"I took a job with a prestigious marketing firm in L.A.," Ruby said. "After spending three years going stark raving mad in a tiny cubicle that for all intents and purposes might as well have been a chicken crate on an egg-laying assembly line, I chucked it all and returned to the roots I'd spurned. You're sure I don't have grease on my face?"

This time Madeline smiled. "I'm positive."

At the city limit sign, Ruby said, "I've done all the talking."

Now the silver car in the mirror was close enough to discern the make and year, close enough to see Riley Merrick behind the wheel.

"I don't mind," Madeline said. "Really. My fiancé once told me I have a face everyone talks to."

She didn't miss Ruby's quick glance at her bare ring finger. "Does your fiancé drive a silver Porsche?"

"No."

Now they were both keeping an eye on the car in the mirror.

"But you know somebody who does." At Madeline's nod, Ruby added, "A friend then?"

"Not exactly," Madeline said as the wrecker crawled through a pothole on its way into the garage's driveway. "He just threw me off some property and accused me of trespassing."

Along with the gift of gab and legs long enough to give Heidi Klum a run for her money, Ruby O'Toole possessed the rare and uncanny ability to move her eyebrows independently of each other. She demonstrated before saying, "I should have let you do the talking."

Madeline looked out the side window to see if Riley would follow her into the parking lot. Ruby leaned ahead to peer around her.

Together, they saw him stop at the curb. He lowered his window and stared at Madeline. Yearning swelled inside her, making it difficult to breathe and impossible to tear her gaze away. She wondered how long she would have sat there if he hadn't broken eye contact. Probably as long as it was going to take the beating rhythm of her heart to return to normal.

"Something tells me you haven't seen the last of him," Ruby said quietly after he'd disappeared around the corner at the end of the block.

She was still making up her mind about that.

Madeline left Red's Garage an hour later with a preliminary quote for the repair of her car, simple walking directions to the Gale Motel six blocks away, and more O'Toole family history—red hair wasn't the only thing that ran in that family. She set off at a fast clip, her tote over one shoulder, her purse over the other, her wheeled suitcase bumping along behind her.

Red O'Toole had cautioned her to keep an eye on the sky. She was more concerned about the Land Rover that was following her. She stepped up her pace and reached into her purse for her cell phone.

"You don't need to call 911," a man with shaggy blond hair said, rather sharply in her opinion, as he pulled up beside her. "Riley sent me."

She tried to recall where she'd seen him. "Why

would he do that?" she asked as she considered flagging down the car approaching from the opposite direction.

"You'll have to ask him."

The approaching car passed while she was foolishly still deciding. Great. Now it was just her and this stranger and her cell phone.

The houses in this part of town sat close together. Their graying porches and brown lawns looked forlorn despite the daffodils blooming along their foundations. Not a single curtain moved, which meant there would be no witnesses. She could practically hear their grumbles if her brothers had to drive all the way up here to identify her body. That lovely thought finally brought her to her senses.

Again, the man spoke before she completed the 911 call. "Riley told me your car broke down and that you could use a ride."

"Like I said," she repeated, "why would Riley do that?"

"Like I said, you'll have to ask him." The guy wasn't going to win any awards for charm. For some reason that made her feel less threatened.

"My name's Kipp Dawson. I'm six-one and go a buck seventy soaking wet. See for yourself." He fumbled through the glove box then held his license toward her. When she failed to move closer, he tossed it to her, wallet and all.

She read his ID while keeping an eye on her surroundings. "What are you doing here, Mr. Dawson?"

"I'm giving you a ride. Unless there's somebody else who can come and get you."

"I have three older brothers. Three *protective* older brothers. Accomplished hunters, all of them."

"If you were going to call them, you would have by now."

In other words, she'd wasted her breath on the implied threat.

"Riley has two brothers," he said as if it had relevance to this conversation. "Half brothers, technically, one older, one younger. Pains in the ass, both of them. They come through for him when it counts, though."

A fat raindrop landed on her forehead while she was wondering why this stranger was sharing Riley's personal information with her. Within seconds the sky opened up, just as Red O'Toole had predicted.

Kipp got out of his vehicle and wrestled her suitcase from her. After tossing it into the back of his aging Land Rover, he said, "Riley has friends, too, who have his back. We're worried about him."

She stood ten feet away in the pouring rain, uncertain what to do about Kipp Dawson and his offer.

"Riley thinks his mother sent you," he said, getting soaked, too. "I talked to Chloe a few minutes ago. She didn't mention you."

Madeline could have blurted the truth, but if she told anyone the reason she was here, it had to be Riley. And she had no right to tell him unless he asked. What had she gotten herself into?

"Maybe having a nurse around isn't such a bad idea," Kipp said.

"Are you saying you think he needs a nurse?" she asked.

"I'm not saying anything. I'm just offering you a ride to the motel because Riley asked me to. Do you want it or don't you?"

Kipp Dawson looked as rough and unkempt as his dented old Land Rover. He was probably right about weighing one-seventy. Men didn't often lie about their weight. His hair appeared darker now that it was wet and his whisker stubble was too straggly to be a fashion statement. Beneath his exterior was a vein of something earnest.

That didn't make him her friend.

She tossed his wallet back to him and continued on her way. Walking faster now that she wasn't weighted down by her cumbersome suitcase, she heard him swear and close his door. Then he was following her again in his car.

The little motel was exactly where Ruby had said it would be. Kipp parked under the portico beneath a lighted vacancy sign that was missing the *C,* then hauled her bulky suitcase out of the backseat. After setting it heavily on the pavement next to her, he got back in the driver's seat without uttering a word.

For some reason she felt compelled to say, "Riley made it clear he doesn't need a nursemaid, as he put it."

Kipp lit a cigarette before replying. "Riley doesn't talk about what he needs. You ask me, a good roll between the sheets with a pretty nurse might be just what the doctor ordered."

Madeline was left staring at his taillights as he drove away, wondering how many more times she would have to consciously close her gaping mouth today.

Sully's Pub began its existence as a boarding-house for lumberjacks in the mid-1800s. The ax and saw marks on the rough-hewn beams over the bar were as evident today as they were in the black-and-white photograph that immortalized Ernest Hemingway having a beer here in 1948. The waitress was a brown-eyed young woman named Sissy. She wore her dark hair short and her T-shirt tight, the words *Yale is for thinkers—Gale is for drinkers* stretched across her chest. According to her, the fine folks of Gale have been hoping to lure someone famous to town ever since. Other celebrities had reportedly purchased property in the area, but if they drank, it wasn't at Sully's.

Madeline hadn't come to Sully's to meet anybody famous. She came because she was starving and the desk clerk at the motel said it was the only place within walking distance that served food this late during the off-season.

The bar was surprisingly crowded on this Friday evening in April. It had a simple menu, small tables, mismatched chairs, paneled walls and one pool table in the back where Madeline and Ruby were losing to a petite brunette named Amanda and her clean-cut accountant boyfriend, Todd.

"You're really going to make me do this, aren't you?" Ruby sputtered to Amanda after scratching on an easy shot.

Amanda didn't let the fact that she was nearly a head shorter than Ruby intimidate her. Crossing her arms stubbornly, she said, "You've been my best friend my entire life and I'm not attending our ten-year high school reunion without you."

Without her ball cap to subdue it, Ruby's wavy red hair fell halfway down her back. Even in flat shoes, her legs looked a mile long. In fact, everything about her was long—her eyelashes, her silences, her sigh before she said, "Pete's going to be there."

"So?" Amanda asked.

"Pete," Ruby said with obvious disdain. "You know. Peter. As in Cheater Peter?"

"You guys finished here?" somebody asked.

After relinquishing the pool table to a group celebrating a twenty-first birthday, Todd said, "Just take a date."

As if it was that easy. "Ugh," was all Ruby said.

Obviously accustomed to these conversations, Todd excused himself and ambled over to talk to someone on the other side of the room. Now that it was just women, Amanda explained Ruby's dilemma to Madeline.

"Sure she could ask Jason Horning, but he's practically eye-level with the girls here." She gestured in the vicinity of Ruby's chest. "And Ruby's always had a thing about short men. I mean, *a thing.* A few years ago, a man escaped from the Benzie County Jail. Every hardware store within fifty miles sold out of dead bolts and buckshot the first day. And do you know what Little Red Riding Hood here said? 'I wonder if he's tall.'"

Even Ruby smiled at the memory, until she said, "Buckshot. Now, there's an idea."

Madeline was so intrigued she didn't notice Sissy's approach until she'd plunked a beer down next to Madeline's right hand. "It's from that sulking Adonis at the bar."

The celebration at the pool table was getting rowdier and the pub more crowded, and yet Madeline found Riley Merrick as if she had a radar lock on him. He'd exchanged his khakis and brown bomber for jeans and a crisp cotton shirt, and sat on a stool facing the mirror behind the bar, his back to her.

"Mr. Porsche, I presume?" Ruby said.

Sissy practically swooned. "He first came in about a year ago. Every month or so he returns. He orders a beer at the bar, talks to whoever happens to be sitting next to him, then leaves. I've seen him propositioned, but I haven't seen him take a woman up on it. The guy couldn't be sexier if he tried. I'm telling you, when a man like that buys a girl a drink, he's either apologizing or interested."

"Which is he?" Amanda asked, scooting her chair closer.

"Maybe both," Ruby said. "He accused Madeline of trespassing and practically threw her off some property earlier."

Ruby, Amanda and Sissy were brimming with curiosity.

"He looks tall," Amanda said. "If you don't go talk to him, Ruby here will."

"Would you stop with the height references already?" Ruby sputtered.

Madeline laughed out loud, and it surprised her. She wanted to grasp these young women's hands and thank them for failing to soften their voices around her. They didn't handle her with kid gloves. Of course, they didn't know her history. That anonymity felt breathtakingly liberating. "Would you excuse me?" she asked, surging to her feet.

She'd changed into boots with heels, snug jeans and a black knit shirt. Several people watched her as she made her way to the bar, but she kept her gaze trained on the man watching in the mirror.

"What are you doing here?" she asked after she'd taken the stool next to Riley.

"I thought it was obvious. I bought you a drink."

Oddly, that gruff tone was as refreshing as Ruby's, Amanda's and Sissy's curiosity had been. Eyeing the drop of condensation trailing down her bottle, she said, "I don't drink."

"Then what are *you* doing here?"

In the mirror she saw Todd slip his arm around Amanda's shoulder. It was such a pure and simple gesture of intimacy it sent an ache to her chest. "I just lost a game of eight ball and it wasn't pretty."

"Losing never is."

Riley was a study in contrasts. He was a risk-taker who didn't like to lose, a wealthy business owner who worked alongside his crew. Practically every guy in the bar had at least a few days' whisker stubble on his face. Riley was clean shaven. His shirt had a designer logo; the beer bottle held loosely in his right hand didn't.

"You shouldn't be drinking," she said.

"You even sound like my mother. I hope she paid you in advance."

Riley seemed accustomed to interference from his mother. It might have annoyed him, but Madeline got the distinct impression it didn't intimidate him. "I told you," she said. "She didn't pay me anything. Are you this distrusting of everyone in the medical field?"

She noticed an easing in his expression and a warming in his eyes, and it occurred to her that he was enjoying himself. Some men puffed up their chests or swaggered in order to be noticed. Riley's self-confidence was more subtle.

Someone jostled her from behind and a loud whooping sounded from the group at the pool table. Three middle-aged men yelled at the ref on a television mounted on the wall, drinks were plunked down, a blender started. Sitting in this bar in this

town of strangers, her elbows on the marred countertop, the heel of one boot hooked over the rung of
her stool, she felt a weight lifting.

"I met a friend of yours today," she said. "Kipp
Dawson could use some training in social graces."

"I'll let you tell him."

She shook her head. "I'm pretty sure he threatened me."

"Kipp threatens everyone."

She found herself staring at Riley's mouth. It was
broad, the lower lip just full enough to entice a second look. "He told me he has your back."

"What else did he say?" he asked.

"I won't repeat it verbatim, but he was very poetic."

He leaned closer, as if to tell her a secret. "The only
time Kipp waxes poetic is when he's referring to sex."

Was he flirting with her? Her heart fluttered
wildly at the thought. "Just so there's no confusion,"
she said, her beer a few inches from her mouth. "I'm
not sleeping with you."

"Madeline?"

They were nearly shoulder to shoulder now, their
bottles raised, gazes locked. "Yes?"

"I didn't ask you to." He took his time taking a
long drink, set his beer back on the bar, then added,
"But I was thinking about it."

Her beer remained suspended in midair. Her mind

remained blank. With two fingers placed gently beneath her chin, Riley closed her mouth for her.

"Once more," she whispered, her heart hammering in her chest, her gaze still on his.

"Pardon me?"

"That's my answer."

"What was the question?" he asked.

"How many more times will my mouth go slack today?"

He didn't quite smile, but she thought he wanted to. Feeling a curious swooping pull in the pit of her stomach, she raised her beer to her lips and drank it down.

Chapter Three

"Are you okay over there?" Riley asked as he backed out of a parking spot behind Sully's.

Huddled low in his passenger seat, Madeline forced her eyes open and tried to focus on the lighted dials on the dash. "It must have been that last margarita."

"More like the last three margaritas," he said. "You and your friends were the life of the party. The bartender said their karaoke machine hasn't seen that much action all year."

She held a hand to her forehead, remembering. Madeline had jumped in to harmonize as Ruby sang the greatest Pat Benatar song of all time, "Hit Me with Your Best Shot."

And somebody had, a shot of tequila for each of them, that is. Things were a little blurry after that. She couldn't quite recall how she came to be missing one earring. Was she wearing Riley's jacket? Where was hers?

Moaning softly, she said, "This is why I don't drink."

"I saw how you don't drink."

She considered telling him a gentleman wouldn't have mentioned that, but then he probably would have said a gentleman hadn't, and she just wasn't up to that kind of banter. When his tires splashed through a pothole, she placed a hand over her poor stomach.

"Hold on," he said. "These streets are coming apart. I can turn the radio on if you think it'll help, but if I go any slower, we'll be moving backward through time, and I doubt you want to relive the past ten minutes."

"What I want is someone to start an IV to put me in a medically induced coma."

"So it's true."

"What's true?" she asked miserably.

"Doctors and nurses make terrible patients."

"To tell you the truth, I've never been a patient."

She paused a moment before broaching a very delicate subject. "What kind of patient were you?"

"The impatient kind, to hear my brothers tell it."

She liked the mellow tone of his voice and the way he didn't take himself too seriously. She wished he would keep talking. "Kipp said you have two brothers."

"Kyle and Braden. Between us we had one father and three mothers, all of whom have a wide array of yappy little dogs that are obnoxiously high-strung, and too many grandmothers and aunts to officially count, most of whom are also obnoxiously high-strung. Kyle calls the women in the family The Sources because they leak information when it suits their hidden agendas. I don't know how much my mother told you about me."

Obviously he hadn't called his mother. If he had, he would know she'd had nothing to do with Madeline's arrival in Gale.

"Riley, she didn't—"

"Why don't you tell me what you already know."

I knew the sound of your heart beating before it was yours, and the way it felt beneath the palm of my hand.

If only she could say that out loud. But she couldn't do that without explaining how she'd discovered his identity.

Her memories of that horrible day never recurred

in their natural order. Instead they flashed back randomly from out of the blue, blindsiding her every time. There was the E.R. doctor's grave expression, the screech of a gurney, the specialist they called in to confer. Dread. Her frantic race to reach Aaron in time, the sting of her own tears. Dread. The discordant hiss and rattle of the machines doing what Aaron could no longer do, the results of the tests, the bitter taste of coffee. Dread.

It went on for hours and hours. Gradually the seconds slowed then stopped altogether. It was over. One moment she'd been saying goodbye, and the next she was engulfed in a void so vast it sucked the air from her lungs, the sound from the room, and color from every surface. Summer believed Madeline had been having a panic attack. Madeline only knew that the pressure building in her chest had forced her from Aaron's bedside and sent her clamoring for the stairs.

Up and around and up and around she'd gone until she'd burst onto the hospital roof where a helicopter was readying for takeoff. She crept close enough to feel the wind from the blades, the *whomp, whomp, whomp* matching the horrible pressure in her chest. The hospital staff scurrying about paid no attention to her. Since she was wearing scrubs, she probably blended right in. She dazedly stepped aside as two men raced toward the helicopter. One carried a cooler; the other was talking on a cell phone.

"ETA one hour," he said as he veered around her. "Prep Riley Merrick for surgery. His new heart is on the way."

The next thing she knew the helicopter was lifting. It hovered overhead, turned then disappeared in the midnight sky. All that remained in the ensuing stillness was the *whomp, whomp, whomp* of her heart and the whisper of Riley Merrick's name.

There were strict laws protecting patients' identity. Even if it was legal, did she have the moral *right* to tell him about Aaron? Transplant recipients were always given the opportunity to obtain information about their donor. If Riley had wanted to know, he would have gone through the proper channels via his surgeon and the hospital. For whatever reason, he hadn't. Madeline didn't see what choice she had but to allow him to continue to assume she was here because of his mother.

"Are you still awake?" Riley asked, bringing her from her reverie. Hearing her sigh, he said, "Why don't you tell me something about you."

Seconds passed while she tried to think of something to say, a place to begin. "I'm normally an open book. My fiancé used to say I told everyone I meet my life story."

"I noticed you aren't wearing a ring," he said. "Who ended it?"

"I guess he did."

"You guess?"

"He died."

This was when most people voiced one of the stock phrases for which there was no response.

I'm so sorry to hear that.

He must have been terribly young.

Time heals.

But Riley asked, "How long were you engaged?"

Concentrating on the blue dash light and the way it illuminated his hands, she said, "I knew I was going to marry him in the fifth grade."

"I thought that only happened in third world countries and biblical times."

In a hundred years Madeline hadn't planned to laugh. Riley rarely said what she expected. The sensation of being caught unawares was new and mildly exciting and other things she would have been able to identify if she hadn't taken her little trip to Margarita-Ville tonight.

Riley was smiling, too. When he looked at her, something changed in the very air she breathed. A delicate connection was forming between them. It sent a flutter of nerves to her stomach and the flutter of something else slightly lower.

They rode the remaining three blocks to the Gale Motel in silence. She got out of the car by rote after he parked, rifled through her purse until she found her key card and arrived at her door at the same time he did. Suddenly she froze.

"Something wrong, Madeline?" His voice was a low vibration that drew her gaze. The light over the door cast half his face in shadow. His hair fell across his forehead and his hands rested lightly on his hips as if he was as comfortable here as he was sitting on a bar stool or walking on narrow beams thirty feet off the ground.

He was good at this.

He leaned closer, not close enough to make her think he might kiss her, but close enough for her to smell his air-cooled skin and beer-warmed breath. Beneath those scents was the living breathing smell of risk.

He didn't touch her—he wasn't quite a rogue. Instead he stayed within reach should *she* choose to touch him—he wasn't quite a saint, either. He was something dangerous in between.

Risk. Danger.

She panicked.

Shoving the key card into the slot, she blurted, "Thanks for the ride. I mean that. Good night, Riley." A second later the door closed behind her.

It wasn't long before she heard a car start. She didn't have to look through the peephole to know he had gone.

Breathing shallowly, she studied her room. Her suitcase was open on the low dresser, her toiletries strewn across the faux marble vanity. She almost didn't recognize her own reflection in the mirror above it—her hair mussed, her face flushed, her lips parted slightly.

What was happening to her?

This trip was supposed to bring her a sense of peace, of completion, of closure. It felt more like a desperate attempt to make sense of something beyond mere mortals' comprehension.

If Aaron were here, he would say, "I told you so."

She missed that about him. She missed everything about him, from the way the sun touched his hair with gold to how his smile lit up his blue eyes. She missed his optimism and the way he always thought the best of everyone. She missed hearing about his students' escapades. She even missed the way he'd cracked his knuckles in church and dumped sugar straight from the sugar bowl into his coffee.

Moving slowly lest she detonated an explosion in the pit of her stomach, she stepped away from the door. She was turning the dead bolt when she noticed she was still wearing Riley's jacket. Emotion swelled inside her as she brought the sleeve to her nose. It was unsettling, for the man stepping boldly into her mind wasn't Aaron—this man had dark wavy hair, deep-set eyes and a stance that had attitude written all over it.

The door to Madeline's room was propped open, a cleaning cart blocking the entrance. Riley stood outside, looking in. The bed was freshly made, ready for the next guest. Madeline was nowhere in sight.

He was too late. She was gone.

Built of cinder block fifty odd years ago, the Gale Motel had a total of eight rooms on one floor. The roof was patched, the windows aluminum factory issue. The place completely lacked architectural appeal. But wild horses couldn't have kept him away this morning.

"I'm too late," he said as he untied the dog's leash from the railing. "The desk clerk said Madeline checked out thirty minutes ago."

The dog stared up at him as if to say, "What are you going to do about it?"

There wasn't much Riley *could* do about it. He didn't know her phone number, where she lived or where she worked. He supposed he could always ask his mother then dismissed the idea as quickly as it formed. He'd had a few beers with a pretty woman. Hours later he'd had one amazing dream about her.

End of story. Certain aspects of the dream still lin-gered in his mind and in his bloodstream, making their brief association feel unfinished, but she was gone, and that was that.

He didn't remember the last time he'd been this preoccupied with a woman he'd just met. She wasn't even his type. Normally he liked his women chesty; surgically enhanced was fine with him. And they wanted what he wanted. Half the time they were the aggressors. Madeline liked him—a man could al-ways tell—and yet she'd ducked into her room last night without so much as a backward glance.

The dog strained against the leash, dragging Riley from his musings. "What is it?" he asked. "What's your hurry?" Normally the old stray poked his nose in a hundred different places. Today he wanted to run.

Riley gave him the lead. They hit Elm Street hard, then Third, and finally the last stretch along Shore-line Drive. They were starting up the driveway when Riley caught a glimpse of Madeline's pale blond hair before she disappeared behind the arborvitae hedge in his backyard.

Well, well, well. She hadn't left town after all.

The dog gave a short bark then tugged against the leash again. "You want to show off for the lady?"

For a mutt, he had good instincts.

"Just remember," Riley said as he matched his pace to the dog's steady run. "I saw her first."

There was one rainstorm every April that spun the seasonal dial to spring. It lightened the sky, mellowed the breeze, gentled the air and left every living organism quivering with irrepressible enthusiasm.

Yesterday's downpour hadn't been that storm.

The pummeling rain *had* given everything in its path a good cleaning and the temperature *was* warmer today. Rooftops, streets, sidewalks, even the boardwalk leading to the lakeshore glistened in the morning sun. Under the surface, the earth was restless. Melancholy. Like Madeline.

She'd forgotten to close the blinds in her room last night and had awakened in the sun-drenched bed, shards of sunlight boring holes through her eye sockets. A quick shower and two aspirin had tamed her headache, thank goodness for small favors. She'd wasted no time packing. She'd checked out of her room, picked up her car and said goodbye to Ruby.

It was time to go home.

She'd accomplished what she'd come to Gale to do, and more. Yesterday she'd seen Riley, she'd spoken with him, she'd even spent a little time with him. No matter what he thought his mother thought he needed, he was obviously physically fit, healthy and strong.

She had only one thing left to do.

With the jacket she'd somehow ended up wearing home last night now folded over her left arm, she pressed Riley's doorbell again.

When she'd picked up her car at Red's Garage, she'd asked Ruby's father if he knew where Riley Merrick lived. Five minutes later she'd driven away with his address, driving directions and a description of Riley's house. Red O'Toole hadn't been exaggerating. Riley's house was a sprawling single story that blended into the surrounding hills. It had a low-pitched roof, deep eaves and wide porches. It wasn't so large that he wouldn't have had ample time to answer the door by now if he was inside.

What now?

She supposed she could have left his jacket on the railing, but she preferred to return it in person. Wondering if he might be down by the lake, she followed an old flagstone path around the house.

The property was amazing, the lawn a gradual slope that leveled off just before it reached the water. Shading her eyes with one hand, she watched a catamaran drift slowly by, its bright orange sail rippling halfheartedly on the melancholy breeze. Several fishing boats trolled back and forth on the horizon, and sea gulls bickered in the foamy shallows.

Riley wasn't back here, either.

Disappointed, she turned and slowly retraced her footsteps. She reached the flagstone path only to stop abruptly.

Riley and a large brown dog were running toward her. Wearing a black T-shirt and loose athletic pants, he stopped twenty feet away and unhooked the dog's leash. While the dog raced to the water's edge to scatter the squawking seagulls, Riley let his hands settle on his hips in a stance she was coming to recognize.

"I rang your doorbell," she said quickly. "And I tried knocking. I wanted to return your jacket before I go."

Breathing heavily but not excessively, he wiped his face with the front of his shirt, giving her a glimpse of a washboard stomach before he said, "The desk clerk said you'd already gone."

"You went to my room?" she asked. "Why?"

"It's a cardinal rule. A guy gets a girl drunk, he buys her breakfast."

She felt a smile coming on and wondered how he did that. "You didn't get me drunk."

"Then I'll *fix* you breakfast instead."

"Do you cook?" she asked.

"That depends. Are you accepting?"

She handed him his jacket and saw no reason not to follow in the direction he was indicating, up the porch steps and through his back door. The dog came in, too, and immediately started drinking from a bowl on the floor.

Madeline looked around the kitchen. With the exception of the stainless steel coffeemaker, the appliances looked as if they'd been new in the sixties. The house seemed even larger from the inside, and had beamed ceilings and hardwood floors and wide archways.

"It's called prairie style," Riley said from a few steps behind her. "It's an original Frank Lloyd Wright house. His open-concept design was way ahead of its time."

She walked as far as the first archway and what appeared to be the living room. She saw richly stained wood, well-crafted built-ins, mullioned windows and a good deal of furniture covered with sheets. "When did you move in?"

"A year and a half ago."

She turned around slowly. The fact that he chose that moment to take a frying pan from a low cabinet and a carton of eggs from the refrigerator might have been a coincidence. But she doubted it.

On the verge of understanding something meaningful about him, she said, "Before or after your heart transplant?"

"Moving into this house was the first constructive thing I did after I left the hospital. I use the kitchen, one bedroom and bathroom. I haven't gotten around to doing much with the rest."

She stored the information, because surely there was something prosaic about the time frame. Watching him crack eggs into a bowl, she said, "Where did you learn to cook?"

"I scramble eggs and sear meat on a charcoal grill. Neither constitutes cooking."

She smiled again, wondered again how he did that.

"Have a seat," he said. "I'll get the orange juice."

The moment she was seated, the dog padded over to be properly petted. His coat was brown but there was gray in his muzzle. Someone had done a poor job of lopping his tail. He wagged it anyway. She found she liked that about him. "What's your dog's name?"

"He isn't my dog."

Rubbing the creature's big knobby head, she said, "Whose dog is he?"

Riley leaned against the countertop behind him. Drying his hands on several paper towels, he watched her pet the dog. The old boy was in seventh heaven. "I have no idea. He scratched on my door three weeks ago, desperate and shivering. His fur was falling out and his ribs were practically poking through his skin."

"You fed him."

Three little words had no business making him feel like some damn hero. Madeline had that effect on him. She was like an elixir for an ailment he couldn't name, and brought out every sexual impulse he had.

She'd fastened her hair high on her head with a silver clip, the ends sticking out in every direction. Wearing a plain white T-shirt and weekend jeans, she couldn't have looked more wholesome if she'd tried. He'd been craving wholesome all morning.

He'd never considered himself the caveman type, but he found himself wondering if the human race might have become a little too civilized. Survival would have been difficult for Neanderthal man, but at least his approach to sex would have been straightforward, requiring only a club and a loincloth.

Seducing modern woman called for a little more finesse.

Riley was warming to the idea of a good challenge. He turned around long enough to drop some butter and the eggs into the frying pan and pour their orange juice, then crossed the room, a glass in each hand.

Madeline smiled a quick thank-you and took a sip of her juice before looking down again where his coffee mug still sat half-full and stone-cold. Tracing one of the scorch marks marring the old hickory surface, she said, "You must wait out a lot of nights here."

She was extremely astute. The truth was, he spent more nights than he cared to think about sitting at this table, quietly draining a pot of steaming coffee one cup at a time as he waited for the stubborn sun to inch into view.

"Nightmares?" she asked.

There was no sense denying it, even though the blasted nightmare hadn't been to blame last night. He'd awakened before 4:00 a.m., the sheet tangled around his waist, his pillow no substitute for the wholesome blonde who'd seemed so wonderfully real until he'd opened his eyes.

He set his juice on the table. Resting lightly on both hands, he leaned closer. Her pupils were dilated in the shadowy room, so that only a narrow ring of blue surrounded them. If she was wearing makeup, it was subtle. Her cheeks looked dewy, her lips pink and so kissable. Before the morning was over, he was going to sample them.

Either she didn't feel the current stretching taut between them, or she refused to acknowledge it. She told him about her parents' deaths when she was twelve, about her older brothers and the family business in a town called Orchard Hill. She didn't broach the subject of her late fiancé, Aaron somebody-or-other.

So Riley did.

"How did he die?" he asked, still leaning on his hands, still thinking about kissing her.

"A motorcycle accident. I'd just started my shift at the hospital when I got the call. A witness said a frazzled young mother late for work crossed the center line. She and her little girl died in the accident. Aaron died twelve hours later."

"Sonofabitch," he said.

Her eyes widened. "How do you do that?" she asked. "How do you make me feel as if you understand me? You don't even know me."

"I know everything I need to know about you."

He had her full attention.

"Do you now," she said.

When her gaze dropped to his mouth, he knew she felt the current, too. "I know you carry a stethoscope in your shoulder bag. I know you were engaged in the fifth grade. You get drunk on three margaritas. And you make a habit of trespassing."

With a small smile, she said, "I was tipsy, not drunk. And I knew I was going to marry Aaron in the fifth grade, but we didn't actually become engaged until years later."

"How long has he been gone?"

She swallowed. "It was a year ago last October."

"Are you seeing anyone now?"

"Of course not."

He didn't bat an eye. The guy had been her first love, probably her only love. Riley wasn't looking to replace a dead man and she wasn't ready to fall in love again. She needed what the talk-show shrinks called a transitional relationship. Since Riley only wanted her in his bed, the sooner the better, this had all the makings of a perfect arrangement.

"Riley?"

"Hmm?" It wasn't easy to drag his gaze away from her mouth.

"Do you smell something?" she asked.

He sniffed.

Just then the smoke alarm shrieked. He raced to the stove as the first flames shot out of the frying pan. He smothered the fire with the lid but there was nothing he could do about the black smoke that escaped in belching clouds. He opened the window and the door then fanned the smoke alarm with a used pizza box.

Creeping closer with the trepidation of a month-old kitten, Madeline peered with him at the charred remains of their omelets. "Does it look done to you?" he asked.

She burst out laughing. Riley couldn't help himself. He threw back his head and joined in.

He roared, she chortled. It had been a long time since either of them had laughed like this, and they wound up holding on to their stomachs, eyes watering, chests heaving, laughing so hard they hurt.

The smoke alarm stopped wailing before their guffaws quieted. In the ensuing silence, he said, "How does cold cereal sound to you?"

It started them both laughing all over again.

"Thank you," she said, wiping tears.

"For what?" he asked.

"I don't know yet." She returned to the table and took another sip of her orange juice. Tracing another scorch mark on the table top with one finger, she said, "This nightmare of yours. Did it start after your heart transplant, too?"

He didn't want to talk about his surgery.

Obviously interpreting his silence accurately, she said, "You might as well just tell me because now I won't be able to stop needling until I know."

Releasing a pent-up breath of frustration, he said, "In the dream, I'm staggering blindly inside a derelict building that seems to go on and on. I have one hand over the gaping hole in my empty chest. With the other hand I'm groping the wall, searching room after room."

Madeline felt her mouth go dry and the blood drain out of her face. "What are you looking for?" she whispered.

A full five seconds passed before he said, "My old heart."

She was in dangerous territory and had been since the conversation began. She knew she wasn't going to like his answer, but, choosing her words carefully, she asked anyway. "Why, Riley? You have a brand-new heart."

He stood a dozen feet away, feet planted, eyes narrowed. She could see a vein pulsing in his neck. And even though he lowered his voice, she heard him say, "Because I liked the old one better."

She didn't pretend to understand the reason bad things happened. Half the time the phases of the moon and the unwritten laws of the universe left her blank and shaken. And yet she knew to her very soul that every choice, every situation, every life had a purpose.

Since Aaron's death, she'd been wondering what her purpose was. Maybe there was a good reason Riley's mother thought he needed a nurse. Maybe he needed to take ownership of his dog, of his house and of his new heart.

Maybe Madeline could help with that.

The thought took hold as she looked at the dog waiting for a name, at the furniture waiting to be unveiled and at Riley waiting for her to say something. Although she had no idea how she was going to accomplish any of this, one thing was certain. Her melancholy mood had completed lifted.

Chapter Four

The more Madeline saw of Riley's house, the more she thought it suited him. Both were classic in design and revealed only a little at a time.

Dust particles floated weightlessly through the air in his living room, catching like faerie dust on the sunbeams slanting through the windows across the room. Madeline didn't need magic to imagine what the room would look like when the sheets were removed and the furniture unveiled.

She and Riley had eaten breakfast standing at the counter in his kitchen, ankles crossed, a bowl of cereal with milk and strawberries in one hand, spoon in the other. Dining this way had become a common practice for her these past eighteen months. Tables were for families. And couples.

They'd talked about the weather and the Detroit Red Wings and a movie star who was in the news again, but she hadn't broached the subject of spending the remainder of her vacation in Gale. And she *wanted* to stay. The realization set off a mild thrum she thought might be gladness.

Already she was formulating a plan.

Riley may not have named his dog, but he treated him well, with a kind word, plenty of food and a soft green pillow next to the stove. In return, the dog adored him. He followed him everywhere and listened with rapt attention as if he understood every word Riley said. Encouraging him to choose a name would be fun. It wouldn't be difficult to remove the remaining dust sheets and rearrange his furniture, either. Riley's recurring dream was Madeline's biggest concern. She wasn't a trained counselor, but she was a good listener. Perhaps talking about it at greater length would help.

When they'd first met at the construction site yesterday he'd assumed she'd been hired by his mother. Madeline couldn't blame him for jumping to conclusions. After all, she *had* wandered onto private property, and apparently Riley's mother often meddled.

Aaron's mom had been the same way. Since her son's death, the lines beside Connie Andrews's mouth had deepened and her eyes had dulled.

Mothers had good reason to worry.

Shaking herself out of her reverie, Madeline tried to pick up the vein of conversation. "Let me get this straight," she said. "You're the middle brother. Braden races boats and is three years younger and Kyle, a journalist, is four years older."

Riley was taking her on a leisurely tour of his house. She wasn't surprised he'd pointed out the more prominent features of the home's horizontal form, the use of wood and stone and symmetry, but she found she was enjoying his anecdotal accounts even more.

"Kyle, Braden and I weren't raised together, per se, but we stuck together out of self-defense," he said as they passed a period bathroom where she saw several pill bottles next to the sink. "Until Kipp came to live with my mother and me when I was fourteen, Kyle, Braden and I were the only males in three households of women. Other than one son apiece and a weakness for our father, the only things our mothers had in common was a mutual love for us, a passion for shopping and small, high-strung dogs. When Braden was ten, one of my mother's Pekingeses latched on to the seat of his pants and wouldn't let go. They had to sedate him."

"Braden?"

"The dog. If you should ever meet my younger brother, don't let him show you his scar."

"Trust me, I can handle gory," she said. "His scar is bad?"

"It's barely visible."

He'd done it again, made her laugh out loud. Their easy camaraderie made her wonder what she was waiting for. "I was thinking," she said. "Since there's no place I have to be until next weekend, I'd like to—"

He turned around slowly, a marvelous shifting of long limbs and masculine ease, and met her smile with an expression that made her aware that they were now in his bedroom. Her heart beat a little faster and her mind went completely blank. She didn't seem to know where to look. Speaking coherently was out of the question. Evidently so was thinking.

Riley could see that Madeline was flustered. Much of what she felt showed on her face. A few minutes ago her blue eyes had darkened with something that had damn little to do with crown molding and original hardwood floors. If he were to harbor a guess, he'd say it was ghosts from the past. What she was feeling now was between the two of them. Something was happening here. There was curiosity, and if he wasn't mistaken, a mutual attraction.

And he was rarely mistaken about that.

As he'd shown her through his house, he'd begun to see it through her eyes. *What are you waiting for?* the untouched rooms seemed to whisper.

The answer eluded him even now.

Before moving in, he'd had the fourth bedroom converted into a master bathroom with heated floors, a steam shower and a bathtub for two. The king-size bed in the adjoining bedroom had down pillows and the most luxuriant cotton sheets money could buy. And yet he'd done very little entertaining here. Other than the few times Kipp had dragged him to a club, Riley had practically been a saint since his surgery.

He watched Madeline open a book he'd been reading. Her lashes looked dark against her pale skin. There was a slight indentation in her chin he hadn't noticed before. He could see the narrow ridge of her collarbone through her white shirt, and a little lower, the edges of her lacy bra. Anticipation stirred in his blood.

His sainthood was on its last leg.

Her gaze found his as he crossed the room. For a moment it was as if she wanted to climb right inside. It was heady, a little like making love without touching.

He wasn't mistaking the mutual attraction.

"You were saying there's no place you have to be

until next weekend," he said, his voice sounding husky in his own ears.

"Yes."

"And?" he asked.

"And I was thinking I'd like to stay here."

The jut of desire settled low and heavy, the temptation to tip her face up for a long, deep kiss growing stronger by the second.

"Not *here* here," she added quickly. "Here in Gale."

He preferred the first here, but here in Gale wasn't a bad second option. "I'd like that."

Madeline didn't know what was wrong with her. There was a humming in her ears and she was acting like an imbecile. She stepped away from him, testing her shaky legs to make certain they would hold her.

He assumed the stance she was coming to recognize, feet apart, hands on his hips, an effortless shifting of muscles and ease that did nothing to restore her equilibrium. "I should be going. Since I'm officially on vacation, I'd like to look for a cute little place to rent, maybe a cottage or a cabin near the water."

"Madeline?" He spoke at the same time his phone rang on the leather-topped desk across the room.

"Take your call," she said. "I'll let myself out."

"Wait." He went to the desk, but instead of answering the phone, he scribbled something on a notepad. "Kipp owns several rentals. He'd probably give you a good deal this early in the season. Here's his cell number. Here's mine, too." He tore the top sheet off and handed it to her. "Call me when you're settled in."

She backed up three steps and managed to leave the room without walking into the wall. She found her way to the kitchen with its marred table and the faint scent of burnt eggs and the quiet echo of shared laughter. She retrieved her shoulder bag from the back of the chair and made a beeline for the door and some much-needed brisk April air.

Ruby was just getting back from her last service call of the morning when Madeline pulled into the parking lot in front of Red's Garage.

"I thought you'd be halfway back to Orchard Hill by now," Ruby said, jumping down from the truck's cab.

"I changed my mind." Madeline got out, too, and closed her car door. "I've decided to stay until the end of the week and I was hoping you'd help me look for a place. To rent. If you're not too busy, I mean. I'll understand if you can't. I can always stay at the Gale Motel. Maybe I'll just go there now."

"Would you breathe?" Ruby whisked her ball cap

from her head and let her curls loose. "I'd love to look at rentals with you."

Madeline relaxed for the first time since setting foot in Riley's bedroom an hour ago. After leaving his house, she'd driven through the quiet streets of Gale, past impressive houses and churches and schools empty on this Saturday afternoon. She drove past Sully's Pub at the end of Main Street and the other businesses that made up the downtown district.

The note bearing Riley's and Kipp Dawson's phone numbers was still in her purse. And it was going to stay there.

She was in mourning—it sounded old-fashioned, but it was true. She doubted she would ever get over losing Aaron, but apparently she wasn't as numb as she'd thought she was. Her heart had sped up beneath Riley's gaze. For just a moment she'd felt—*gulp*—attracted to him. She'd panicked. Her stomach still did a somersault when she thought about it.

Driving aimlessly had helped put her reaction in perspective. She was human. And humans felt. Emotions, reactions, responses, things they were better off not feeling. It didn't have to mean anything. She liked Riley, and she wanted him to be happy. She wanted everyone to be happy. She couldn't be completely honest with him about her reasons for coming to Gale. She also couldn't sit idly by while he got the wrong idea about her intentions. She'd decided the best way to keep a respectable distance was to find her own place to stay this week.

According to Ruby, there were dozens of cabins and cottages available so early in the season. Together they'd consulted the classifieds in the newspaper and online. They made several phone calls and compiled a list right there in the garage. Ruby's enthusiasm was a balm. Madeline was doing the right thing. Coming to Gale, finding Riley, deciding to spend the week here so she could help him in some small way, it all felt right again, like the marvelous discovery of something as essential to life as air and water.

Two hours and five appointments to look at rentals later, she was wondering if she should have done this alone. Not because Ruby talked a mile a minute—Madeline enjoyed that, but because "You can do better than that," seemed to be Ruby's mantra.

Personally, Madeline would have been satisfied to rent the second-floor efficiency over Red's Garage or the attic in the house near the dunes, but Ruby had other ideas. "You haven't had a vacation in forever," she said. "No *it'll do* rental for you."

So far they'd checked five "it'll do" rentals off the list. Now Madeline was driving again and Ruby was directing her to turn right and left and left again.

"What do you think?" Ruby asked.

Madeline had followed Ruby's directions through narrow lanes and back alleys. They'd taken shortcuts that crisscrossed the hills near Lake Michigan until Madeline had no idea where she was. "I think I'm thoroughly lost."

"Look." Ruby pointed straight ahead.

A quaint little cottage sat at the end of a narrow lane that served as the driveway. The lot was small and lined on three sides by pine trees and arborvitae hedges. The lake glistened gray-blue in the distance and sea gulls glided overhead.

The cottage reminded Madeline of the ones children drew on construction paper. It had a roof pointed like a hat, a crooked brick chimney, two large windows that could have been eyes and a plain front door. A square for-rent sign with faded blue lettering leaned against the steps. The smoke curling from the chimney made it appear lived in.

"Did the owner say how much?" Madeline asked.

"The phone reception was patchy. The guy I talked to said he'd meet us here at two. We're early." Ruby opened her door and swung out.

"Where are you going?"

"To look in the windows. Are you coming?"

Ruby was peering through the low window to the right of the front door when Madeline joined her. They stood out of the wind, the sun directly overhead, their hands cupped beside their eyes like field glasses.

"I like it," Madeline said. "As long as it isn't too expensive, I think this could be the one."

"This change of heart you've had about staying," Ruby said, moving to the other window. "It wouldn't have anything to do with that gorgeous guy who accused you of trespassing then took you home last night. Oh, look, there's a wood-burning fireplace."

Madeline changed windows, too. "It's not what you think. Riley, that's his name, has this mongrel dog he hasn't named and this great Frank Lloyd Wright house he barely lives in. I think I can help."

Ruby looked at her as if she was waiting for the rest of the story. Madeline found herself confessing something she hadn't said out loud to anyone. "I just—I don't know—I guess I don't want to go home yet. Don't get me wrong. Everyone back home is wonderful. They are. I love them to pieces, but ever since Aaron died—Aaron was my fiancé. He died. I still can't believe it, but he did, he died, and now everyone is worried about me. The mailman, the mayor, the clerk in the grocery store, my brothers and the other nurses at work, they all pat my shoulder when they talk to me, and they watch me as if they're afraid I might jump off a bridge or shave my eyebrows the way the ancient Egyptians did when the family cat died."

"They shaved their eyebrows?" Ruby asked. "Really? That seems a little extreme, don't you think? I guess I'm more of a dog person."

Madeline blinked then giggled. *Something must be in the air here.* She was still smiling when she resumed looking in the window. It did have a nice fireplace.

"Trespassing again, I see." The voice was deep and came from directly behind them.

They both let out a gasp as they spun around. Riley and his dog stood a dozen feet away.

"She has an appointment," Ruby said defensively.

"For two o'clock," he said. "Yes, I know."

He knew? Madeline thought. But how? Realization dawned. "You own this cottage."

"You're the guy with the Porsche from the bar last night," Ruby said at the same time.

Riley looked at both of them but spoke to Madeline. "I didn't think you'd want to stay in my cottage, so I gave you Kipp's number."

"Why wouldn't she want to stay in your cottage?" Ruby asked.

This time he looked only at Madeline when he replied. "You strike me as the kind of woman who likes to do things her way."

Again Madeline wondered how he did that. How did he make her feel as if he knew her?

Wearing a long-sleeved shirt but no jacket, he

slipped his hand into the pocket of a pair of Levis just tight enough to be interesting. "Oh my," Ruby said as he brought out a key.

Madeline must have put her hand out to accept the key, because she could feel the edges biting into the palm of her fisted hand. She was glad he didn't seem to expect her to say anything.

The breeze lifted his wavy hair and fluttered through his shirt. Seemingly unfazed by the chill in the air, he said, "I turned the heat on inside the cottage in case you decide you like it."

"Where's your car?" Madeline asked.

"It's parked in my driveway next door."

"We're on Shoreline Drive?" Madeline asked. Earlier, when Red O'Toole had graciously imparted description of and directions to Riley's house he hadn't mentioned an adjoining property.

"Yes," Riley said. "I thought you knew that."

"I guess I'm a little lost," Madeline countered.

Ruby felt as if she was watching a tennis match.

"I've gotta go. Our newest clients have decided they want a glass floor in the foyer. Under the glass they want to display an antique car, but not just any antique car. They have their hearts set on a Riker and they expect me to find one. Kipp has a lead on a Riker belonging to a collector in Charlevoix. He's waiting for me at his place. Go on in and take a look at the cottage. If you like it, make yourself at home. If you don't, just lock the door when you leave."

He took three steps, the dog right beside him. "Oh." Turning again, he said, "Could he stay with you until I get back? I shouldn't be late."

Ruby didn't see Madeline nod, but she must have, because she was holding the leash after he was gone. They both stared at the empty gap in the arborvitae hedge, hearing the screech of gulls overhead, the lap of water in the distance.

"What just happened?" Madeline asked dazedly.

"Apparently you're dog sitting for the rest of the afternoon."

The dog let out a sorrowful howl that raised goose bumps on Ruby's arms. The brown mongrel seemed upset to be separated from Riley.

"Don't worry," Madeline was saying gently. "He'll be back."

He yowled again, a solemn, somber sound.

Ruby looked over at Madeline. She was pale and slender and seemed a little sad. No matter what she said, there was more to her visit to Gale than mourning a beloved fiancé, naming a stray dog and moving some furniture, but she had resiliency, pluck and determination. She was going to be all right.

Ruby wondered if the same could be said for

Riley Merrick. The dog yowled again. Apparently
Ruby wasn't the only one who thought so.

Madeline didn't know where she was when she
opened her eyes. There was a pillow beneath her
cheek, a warm throw over her legs and shoulders, and
an expanse of creamy white directly in front of her
eyes.

Outside the wind seemed to exhale. Inside a clock
ticked. She must have fallen asleep.

Now she remembered. She'd been dog sitting.
She'd stretched out on the sofa in the cottage to wait
for Riley to return. He must have run into trouble,
because darkness had fallen and he still wasn't back.

She snuggled deeper into the warmth of the throw.

Her eyes popped open. She hadn't been covered
up when she laid down. Hurriedly sitting up and
whisking the throw off, she caught Riley and the dog
on their way out. "Going somewhere?" she asked.

He glanced over his shoulder at her, his hand on
the doorknob. "I didn't mean to wake you."

"You didn't." The quiet cadence of their voices
lent an intimacy to the exchange. "I'm surprised I
didn't hear you come in. I'm not normally a sound
sleeper." She stood and instantly curled her bare toes
in the plush rug beneath her feet. "Having your dog
here must have made me feel safe." She looked at the

dog staring back at her from the vicinity of Riley's knee. "Obviously it was a false sense of security. You could have barked," she said, giving the dog's head a gentle pat. "What time is it?"

"It's almost midnight. I didn't expect it to take so long to close the deal on the car. I apologize."

"I didn't mind," she said, and she meant it. "We shared an order of Chung Du Chicken and fried rice, and then he kept me company while I unpacked."

"So you like it?" He gestured around the room with his free hand.

She nodded. The cottage was small but comfortable. Decorated in shades of white, cream and blue, it reminded her of the dunes and the lake and the sky. "Who did your decorating?"

"My stepmother. She wanted to do my house, too, but had to be satisfied with the guesthouse for now. Gwen was afraid, if left to my own devices, there would be leather couches and a big-screen TV."

If he'd intended to make her smile, it worked. He had a shadow of a beard tonight. His sleeves were rolled up and he'd run his fingers through his hair. His quietude was probably a result of fatigue.

"I must warn you," she said, "I have every intention of finding a name for your dog and unveiling your furniture. He looks a little like a Jake, doesn't he?"

Riley shifted his stance and took his hand from the doorknob.

"No?" she asked. "Rocky? Archie. Buster."

He must have noticed her rubbing her upper arms, because he reached to the thermostat to the right of the door and turned up the heat. The dog yawned, prompting her to say, "Droopy? Gumball."

Ruby had said she hadn't heard of anyone who'd lost a dog, but since she'd only recently moved back to Gale, she and Madeline had decided to consult an expert. Ruby's father, Red O'Toole, professed to know everybody in the county, but he hadn't heard of anyone who was missing a dog, either. He hadn't seen any lost-dog posters, and he would have remembered if somebody had posted a reward, which brought up another point.

"If you really had no intention of keeping him, you would have put up found-dog signs. Banjo?" she asked on a small victorious smile. "Spike? Goofy? Rover."

"Madeline, he has a name."

She started. "He does?" And then, after his meaning soaked in, she said, "He probably had a name once, but we don't know what it is. Was. He needs a new one. What about Skeeter? Charlie. King."

Nothing.

"Bubba. Radar?"

More nothing.

"Ajax. Lucky. Rufus?"

Even Riley couldn't help smiling at that last one. He wondered how long it would take her to run out of suggestions.

Despite the apparent normalcy in the room, there was a current on the air, the thrum of something untried and appealing. He knew what he wanted, had known it from the moment he'd covered Madeline with that throw. It hadn't been easy to back away.

Ordinarily, Riley would have been enthusiastic about today's transaction. He'd never seen a more impressive collection of vintage cars. The owner had enthusiastically shared the history and story behind every one. Yet Riley had wanted to make the damn deal and get back to Gale.

Because Madeline was here.

She looked so tempting standing across the room right now, all sleepy-eyed and tousled, her hair in her face, her shirt wrinkled, her feet bare. He stayed near the door because if he came closer, he would reach for her. And it was too soon for that.

"If you want to spend your vacation uncovering my furniture," he said a little more gruffly than he'd intended, "fine. But I'm not keeping this dog."

She must have heard the steel in his voice, because she said, "Why?"

He didn't have to explain himself to her, but it had

to do with the pills he swallowed every day, and the reality always lurking. *Rejection.* Graft-versus-host disease, it was called. It was always possible and always ugly. The second scenario was slightly better, although the side effects to the drugs would eventually take their toll. It wasn't something he liked to think about and he sure as hell didn't talk about it, especially when there was something so much more invigorating happening right here in this very room.

"Maybe I *should* put up signs," he said. "Maybe place an ad online and in the paper, too, if you think it'll do any good."

"You're serious?" she asked.

Her disappointment was palpable. She went to the table with obvious reluctance and began rummaging through her big shoulder bag again. This time she brought out a camera.

"What are you doing?" he asked.

She snapped three pictures in quick succession. "I'm taking pictures for the ad. If you must know, I think you're making a huge mistake."

"No," he said.

"What?"

"No photographs."

"Why on earth not?" she asked.

"Look at him. Why spoil his chances?"

Madeline looked at the dog and then at the

pictures of him in the digital camera's memory. Granted, he wasn't small and cute or sleek and beautiful, but most dog lovers didn't care what a dog looked like. Everything they needed to know could be seen in a creature's eyes. And this dog's eyes were serious and wise.

No matter what Riley said, he didn't want to include a photo because he didn't want anyone else to claim his dog. She didn't know why he wouldn't admit it, but she knew better than anybody that not everything had a simple explanation. Sometimes reasons were hidden, sometimes circumstances were extenuating.

He liked this dog. There was no doubt about that.

She practically ran across the room and didn't stop until her bare toes were almost touching the tips of his shoes. "I'm onto you, Riley Merrick." Reaching up on tiptoe, she kissed his cheek.

He turned his head at the last second, so that her lips grazed his mouth. Her breath caught and her eyelashes flew up. His pupils were dilated in the shadowy room, so that his eyes looked darker. His jaw was set, the shallow cleft in his chin made more pronounced by the shadow of a day old beard.

She drew away slowly, her heart beating too fast and her breathing almost nonexistent. "I don't want to start something," she whispered.

"I know," he said, still holding her gaze. "I'll see you in the morning."

Riley opened the door but waited to leave until he heard the scrape of the dead bolt. The dog sniffed the air on the way back to their side of the hedge. He took care of business then joined Riley on the covered porch.

Once inside, he and the dog followed their usual routine. The dog turned around three times before laying down on the pillow by the stove. Riley stopped in the main bathroom as he did twice every day. He opened the lids on the pill bottles and shook out the proper dosage of each. He swallowed the entire fistful at once. After washing them down with tap water, he wiped his mouth on the back of his hand. All the while he stared at his reflection.

He could still feel the whisper of Madeline's lips against his, could still smell the scent of her shampoo, and still remembered the surprise in her eyes. *I don't want to start something,* she'd said.

It was too late. Something already had.

Chapter Five

The weatherman promised a sunny day.

Madeline scanned the dome of clouds overhead. Tugging the edges of her sweater together, she trudged down the sidewalk beside Riley. No, she refused to trudge. That would have suggested surliness.

Riley stopped in front of a utility pole on the corner of the busiest intersection in Gale and held out his hand. She didn't have much choice but to give him one of the neon yellow flyers with the dark brown lettering.

FOUND: DOG
Friendly brown male
Vicinity of
Shoreline Dr. & 3rd
Call 555-630-1022

What if he'd run away for a reason? She wished she'd never brought up the idea for the signs.

After Riley had left last night, she'd paced from one end of the cottage to the other. She'd told herself that she'd imagined the heat in his eyes before he'd walked out the door, and that her heart didn't teeter sideways when her lips had brushed his. She hadn't fooled herself, though.

When she'd finally gone to bed, she'd wanted so badly to dream of Aaron. Instead, she'd lain awake on the first official night of her vacation, listening to the wind croon and the water wash ashore.

It was getting more difficult to picture him in her mind. Aaron was snow cones and porch swings, slow dancing and knock-knock jokes. He'd been her lab partner in chemistry class and her date to every prom. They'd celebrated together when she'd passed her state boards and he landed his first teaching job. They'd been in step, in sync, in tune, in love.

She and Riley were nothing alike. She never knew

what *he* was going to say, let alone what he was thinking. He was a lightning strike, a riptide, and a sonic boom all rolled into one.

Last night, he'd made her want things she didn't want to want. Her stomach twisted on the truth even now.

I'll see you in the morning, he'd said, but she hadn't gone looking for him today. She hadn't been ready to see him again. Instead, she'd set out for a nice, mind-clearing walk. She made it to the end of the driveway before she ran into him, his posters under one arm and the dog on the green leash. Of course they were going her way.

Her timing was pitiful.

With a sigh, she studied Riley's handiwork now affixed to the wooden utility poll. The poster was easy to read and would be difficult to overlook. It was even laminated in case it rained. Next to her, the somber dog looked on.

Out of the corner of his eye, Riley saw Madeline bend down and cover the dog's eyes. He felt a smile coming on.

"Do you think he can read?" he asked.

He was glad looks couldn't really kill. He grinned, which didn't help at all.

She was cross today. He didn't mind cross. In fact, he had a deep and abiding respect for the condition. A little heat under the collar was a sign of passion, and he would have to be a fool to mind that.

Her light blue sweater was belted at her waist, her cream-colored slacks snug enough to showcase a damned nice derriere. He didn't pretend to understand women's love affair with shoes but he appreciated what Madeline's heels did for an already appealing bit of anatomy.

He'd slept late for the first time in months. Church bells had been chiming when he'd rolled over in his king-size bed. He'd wished she was there.

If it had been any other woman, he would have called her, or better yet shown up with breakfast and let nature take its course. But she wasn't any other woman. She'd been through hell and was just beginning to laugh again. Any sudden moves would send her running. Rather than risk that, he'd decided to take the dog for a walk. Lo and behold, he'd met her at the end of her driveway.

His timing couldn't have been more perfect.

"If you're not a morning person, I respect that," he said after pinning the last poster to the community bulletin board next to the library. "But if you're just having a bad day, having a little fun is good for what ails you."

Madeline stopped so quickly the couple behind her had to veer around her to keep from running into her.

Riley waited for her out of the wind as if he had all the time in the world. "Something wrong?" he asked.

"Don't mind me, I'm having a revelation."

"Take your time."

Oh, that brash self-confidence, she thought. He wore black chinos today and a shirt in a fine, woven broadcloth the same shade of gray as the clouds. The spring in his step, the light in his eyes, and the grin lurking around the corners of his mouth, it was all fitting together in her mind. "You didn't have the nightmare last night, did you?"

"The nightmare, no."

Some might insist it was a coincidence that he'd stopped having the dream after she'd arrived in Gale. It was easier to believe in a divine order when goods things were occurring. The bad experiences were harder to understand. She didn't have to understand everything. Some things, she had to simply accept. Perhaps this was one of those things.

Feeling a little more lighthearted herself, she said, "For months, my best friend has been telling me I need to have more fun."

"No one can tell you how much fun to have. Me? I have standards and limits."

"What kind of limits?" she couldn't help asking.

"I never do anything I wouldn't want to have to try to explain to the paramedics."

His tone was teasing but somehow she believed there was a grain of truth in what he'd said.

"Aren't you going to ask about my standards?" he asked.

With a start she realized he'd caught her staring. She tried to look away, but couldn't. She was reminded of last night when he'd stood in her living room, his eyes heavy-lidded, his voice deep, his jaw darkened with a day-old beard.

"Not on your life," she said.

"In that case, how about lunch?"

The scents of herbed butter and sautéed mushrooms wafted on the air as Madeline and Riley left the restaurant an hour later. Tucked on the hill between First Street and Shoreline Drive, Fiona's Bistro had round tables and white linens, rough plastered walls and polished wood floors. The food was superb.

In her mid-thirties, Fiona herself had stopped by their table. She had dark hair and hazel eyes, wore large diamonds in her ears and had a figure that strained the buttons on her white French blouse. "Hello, Riley," she'd said with a sultry French accent. "Is everything to your liking?"

He'd let his gaze light on Madeline as he said, "As a matter of fact, it is."

Madeline had wanted to nudge him under the table.

"The woman's in love with you!" she told him now as they waited for a car to pass so they could cross the street.

"I highly doubt that," he said.

"I didn't see any dogs lying under anyone else's table. Obviously she's willing to make an exception for you."

"Kipp and I did the renovations on the building two years ago," he said. "I haven't been back since I moved to Gale."

"Maybe you should."

He said nothing, and Madeline wondered if he'd ever been in love. Somehow she doubted it. If he had, he would know that loving someone wasn't a conscious decision. It wasn't even a choice. Sighing, she found herself wanting to fill the ensuing silence.

"You could have been anything. Why architecture?"

"I like houses. No matter how grand the mansion or humble the hut, each begins with walls and a roof. The construction process involves basic physics, joinery and craftsmanship, but there's a point when a house becomes more than the components of its parts." He looked at her, and didn't continue until she looked back at him. "When it's right, it feels right. You know it the way you know to breathe."

Swallowing audibly, she said, "You're passionate about everything, your car, your food, your career."

"And you're not?" he asked.

"I like what I do, but I chose nursing because it's safe." It was true. It was just one of the decisions she and Aaron had made together. He would be a teacher. She would be a nurse. They would graduate from high school with honors, finish college, save for a house, plan their wedding, and someday have children, preferably a boy and a girl. Those dreams crashed down around them before either of them turned twenty-four.

"I'm definitely not a risk-taker, and I don't want you to think—"

He took her hand, stopping her in midsentence. "I don't know what you were like before I met you, but you took a risk when you burst through the gate at the construction site Friday. How many times have you thrown caution to the wind since? You asked me about Fiona. She's pleasant, but she wanted a commitment, and I'm not good at forever. You're staying five more days. It's up to us how far we take this attraction while you're here."

He looked at her, and she knew. He was going to kiss her.

He tipped her head back with one finger and brought his mouth to hers. The instant their lips touched, the kiss spun into a roller coaster ride of sensation.

She'd expected his kiss to be polished and calculated, a process to get from point A to point C. There was no point A. There was only a mating of lips and air and instinct. It was a blending, a melding of holding on and letting go. It was need in the present moment, and it was potent.

His lips were firm, the kiss wet and wild and a little rough on noses and chins. They simply adjusted the angle and opened their mouths, setting their moans free.

When it was over, she held perfectly still. Her knees didn't give out and the earth didn't move, but she knew that what he'd said was true. The connection between them was alive.

She backed up, swallowed. Her breath seemed to have solidified in her throat. She hadn't been kissed in a long time. And never quite like this. "I shouldn't have come here."

"I disagree."

Of course he did. When had he ever agreed with anything she'd said? "I should go home."

"It's only five days, Madeline. If you leave, you'll never know what would have happened during those five days."

He started for the arborvitae hedge, calling the dog as he went. She remained where she was until the pair of them disappeared on the other side. They didn't look back.

She wondered how it would feel to be so sure of something. She used to be that sure. That felt like another woman's life.

Shaken, she went in through the cottage's front door. Slowly turning in a circle, she sank to the sofa, only to jump up again. She ran into the bedroom and dropped onto all fours. She hauled her suitcase out from under the bed, then heaved it onto the mattress and unzipped it as if it was somehow at fault. She yanked the closet open and tossed the only dress she'd brought with her into the open suitcase on the bed. Her slicker went in next. Something fell from the pocket and fluttered to the floor.

Aaron lay staring up at her.

She went utterly still for a moment. Her heart constricted and her lips quivered. It was the last photograph she'd taken of him. He'd been late for school, but had turned when she'd called his name. There was liveliness in his blue eyes. It was the last time she would ever see him smile.

She scooped the photo off the floor and made a run for the back door. She didn't stop until the heels of her shoes sank into the wet sand at the water's edge.

Heart aching, she stared into the distance. The lake was blue and empty today, and so mighty, eighty miles across. Overhead the dome of clouds was lifting. The weatherman had been right. It was going to be a sunny day.

She fell to her knees, and the tears that had been welling ran down her face. They burned her eyes, caught in her mouth, and gathered at her jaw before dropping onto the wet sand.

She wrapped her arms around herself. Rocking back and forth, she let it out, every futile wish, everything it did no good to say.

She cried for Aaron and for all their plans, for the wedding that never occurred and the babies that would never be born. He'd never met her mom and dad. It seemed impossible, but their paths never crossed on this earth. She wanted things to be different. She wanted Aaron to be here, and she wanted her parents to know him. She wanted so badly to say, "Mama, it isn't fair."

It wasn't fair.

None of it was fair.

Every so often somebody back home reminisced about how excited her mom and dad had been when the doctor had said, "It's a girl!" After having three boys, they'd imagined sugar and spice and everything nice. Instead their little darling had been a complete tomboy with pigtails, skinned knees and thin excuses. If it had branches Madeline climbed it, if it had a tail she rode it, and if it was forbidden, she wanted it.

Her hand went to her mouth.

She hadn't thought about her early years in a long time. She remembered the day she'd stopped climbing trees, the day she chose an orderly life over mischief. It was after her parents' icy pile-up on the freeway that fated February day when she was twelve years old. Marsh had moved back home and he and Reed took over the orchard and raising her and Noah. About that time Aaron took the vacant desk next to hers in homeroom in the seventh grade. What began as a friendship in the fifth grade instantly bloomed into a budding first love.

She cried harder than ever, raw, wrenching sobs that hurt her throat and her ribs and stomach. She didn't want her relationship with Aaron to have been the result of her need for something solid. He'd been the love of her life, the other half of her whole. He had.

Yes, he had.

She felt the warm body at her side before she saw him. Although the dog made no sound, she wasn't afraid. He gave her time to adjust to his presence then sidled closer.

"Did Riley let you out?" she asked on a whimper.

Smelling of dog shampoo and lake water, he let her put her arms around him, offering his warmth, asking for nothing. As she laid her cheek on the thick fur on his back, she caught a glimpse of Riley retreat-

ing from view. He'd done more than let the dog out.
He'd sent him to her.

Another tear fell. It hurt, kindness.

"If he's so wise," she said to the dog, "why won't
he give you a name?"

Why did it matter so much to her?

Because. He was alive. And she wanted him to be
glad he was. She wanted him to embrace his life and
his home and his dog.

She sniffled and sighed. "I need a tissue. And you
deserve a treat."

She kissed the dog on the top of his head. Breathing a little better, she stood. It took a few moments
to keep her knees from wobbling. Depleted and
spent, she slowly walked inside her cottage.

Riley was at the door when the dog scratched an
hour later. He let him in, disappointed to find him alone.

Damn.

He'd dealt with females' tears all his life. The
women in his family cried easily, lustily and often.
Madeline's tears had nearly undone him. He'd
wanted to go to her, and had reached the place where
the properties joined when he'd questioned his right
to intrude on something so personal and private. He
didn't want to leave her alone, either. In the end,
he'd sent the dog, instead.

Evidently she'd appreciated the dog's company. If Riley wasn't mistaken, there were cookie crumbs in the fur around the old boy's muzzle. Riley was more interested in the envelope tucked under the dog's collar. He slipped the note out, opened the flap and removed the paper he hoped didn't include goodbye.

Five days. Don't let it go to your head.
I'm thinking maybe Miles. Rocket.
I know. Rex.

The woman didn't give up. They had that in common.

He flattened the note and read it again. She wrote in cursive. Nobody did that anymore. Her handwriting was feminine without being overly ornate. She certainly wasn't wordy.

He brought the stationery to his nose, and found that it wasn't scented. Of course it wasn't. She wasn't the pursuer here.

But she was staying for five days. Five days meant five nights.

From some place far away came the primitive pounding of ancient drums. The resonating echo started in his extremities, inching through his veins toward the center of him where echo and instinct converged.

A tentative knock sounded on his back door. He

tucked the note behind the coffeemaker for safe keeping and went to the door to let Madeline in. Five days had just begun.

"Okay, let's see what's under this one." Madeline whisked a dust sheet off another sofa. "Oh."

Yes, oh, Riley thought as he added another sheet to the growing bundle in his arms. The sofa she'd uncovered was orange and green and couldn't have been attractive when it was brand-new. It hadn't improved with age.

It had been an hour since Madeline had knocked on his door. "Ready to get started?" she'd asked.

He'd been ready since he met her, but she was referring to her project. She was organized, he'd give her that. The Duncan Fife dining set had been revealed, along with most of the furniture in the living room and one of the spare bedrooms. There was dust on her sleeve and a hole in the knee of her faded jeans. Her hair was slightly mussed and her blue eyes had a glassy quality.

He hadn't mentioned her tears and neither had she. She hadn't mentioned the note, either, or the fact that her voice trailed off whenever their hands happened to touch.

"Some of this furniture should probably go." When he didn't reply, she said, "Don't you agree?"

"Agreeable is my middle name."

She made a sound through her pursed lips a man could never replicate. Watching her do it reminded him of her kiss. Breathing reminded him of her kiss.

"Before I risk insulting you, I should ask if any of this was yours before you bought this house."

"Now you're worried about insulting me?" he asked. When she smiled, a weight lifted. It made him feel like a damn hero again.

Apparently she wanted to talk, to slow this down. Slow wasn't his preferred speed, but he could be accommodating. They could talk.

For now.

"Before I moved here, Kipp and I traveled light. We liked to say neither of us accumulated anything that didn't fit into a duffel bag. We specialize in large summer houses, mansions and additions that quadruple the living space for the wealthy. Now we keep an office in Traverse City and employ an accountant and office manager. These days we always have two or three projects running simultaneously, but back then we built our reputation one house at a time and lived in whatever city we worked. We spent an entire year restoring two old inns on Mackinaw Island, but our first major success was a nineteenth-century style English manor on the Grand River in Lansing. The most difficult project to orchestrate was the castle we built for an eccentric dot-com millionaire in Kalamazoo."

Madeline tried to imagine going from town to town, city to city that way. Summer said there were two categories of people: those who were like tumbleweed and those who were trees. Trees put down roots and reached up. Tumbleweed rolled across the surface of the earth, going where the wind blew.

She removed another sheet and carefully added it to the heap in his arms. As it started to slide off, he shuffled the whole bundle, but gravity was winning. She tried to help by gathering up the loose ends and tucking them into the folds. The action brought her closer to him, her hands sliding through the flimsy fabric to the solid man underneath.

His skin was warm beneath her palms, his torso solid, the muscles underneath washboard-strong. Dust particles glittered all around them, and yet he smelled like the outdoors.

He must have let go of the bundle, because she felt the rest of the sheets tumble down around their feet. Free, his hands went to her upper arms, drawing her closer.

His body made contact, key contact with hers, arms, chest, hips and thighs. Heat poured through her, unfurling a yearning so intense it shook her in its throes.

She stared into his eyes, and slowly drew away. "I think that's enough uncovering for this afternoon." She pointed her finger at him. "You know what I mean."

As one second followed another, his expression changed. He probably disagreed again, but he wasn't pressuring her.

"What would you like to do?" he asked.

"Do?"

The heat in his eyes hadn't diminished. It just moved over to make room for whatever risk he was about to suggest.

"I know just the thing," he said. "Let's have some fun."

"Fun is my middle name."

He chuckled as he took her hand, pulling her along with him to the kitchen. She grabbed her shoulder bag from the hook on her way by. He left the dog sleeping in the corner and she left her blue sweater on the back of a kitchen chair.

Outside she had to run to keep up with him.

"Can you drive a stick shift?" he asked.

"Have I mentioned that I have three older brothers?"

He tossed her the keys to his Porsche.

"Where are we going?" she asked, looking at him over the roof of his silver car.

"Wherever you want."

The idea of going anyplace she wanted sent her imagination spinning. "There's a lighthouse near Traverse City we visited when I was little. I've always wanted to go back."

He pointed east. "Traverse City is that way."

She got in, moved the seat up, adjusted her seat belt, and turned the key. She backed around and drove to the end of his driveway. She looked both ways before pulling out then ran through the gears, testing the sound of the engine and the feel of the clutch and the gears and the steering wheel.

"I thought you said you could drive a stick," he said.

"I can drive a manual transmission, Marsh's old jeep and Reed's speedboat. The only thing I haven't attempted is Noah's airplane."

"Put some muscle into that gas pedal," he said. "There's more than one way to fly."

She pushed on the accelerator and the car shot forward, the velocity pressing her deeper into her bucket seat. It did feel a little like flying. Keeping to the speed limit, but barely, she settled in, both hands on the wheel, and drove, just drove. Sometimes they talked, but most of the time they enjoyed a companionable silence. At some point Riley must have put in a CD, for Leonard Cohen's crooning melodies filled the air.

The car sat close the ground, the tires hugging the

pavement around banked curves and over sun-kissed hills and towering cedars. They glided past mossy walls where the highway cut through solid rock. She followed Sunday drivers, and when it was safe, she passed them, music and glimpses of blue water blending the way her tears and lake sand had, the way loss was being absorbed into this airy sense of discovery.

She didn't know how long she drove, but the shadows had lengthened. Traffic had thinned. She didn't remember when she'd last seen a car.

She pulled off the road and coasted to a stop near a scenic overlook. "I must have missed the exit."

"By fifty miles."

For a moment she merely stared, tongue-tied. "Why didn't you stop me?"

"I don't want to stop you."

His eyes were a deep, dark brown, his voice a husky baritone that caused that glorious swooping in the pit of her stomach again. Yesterday she'd felt purged by laughter. Earlier today it had been by tears. This was freedom, and it felt like the greatest risk of all.

"Where exactly are we?" she asked.

"We're not far from Charlevoix. Twenty miles in that direction is St. James on Beaver Island," he said, pointing across the water. "I didn't know the ferry ran this late in the day."

The dome light flickered as she opened the door.

"We've come this far. We might as well not waste that view."

She was out of the car when Riley's phone rang. She glanced back as he checked his caller ID.

"Your L.A. clients again?"

"No, it's my mother."

Madeline was surprised he didn't hear the sharp breath she took. If he'd glanced up, he would have seen her face go pale, but he wasn't looking at her. He was looking at his phone.

Leaving him to his call, she walked along the curved path to the railing. An uneasy feeling followed her all the way.

Long yellow rays of sunlight angled through the pine trees, glinting off the lake. In six weeks the entire area would be teeming with vacationers, hikers and boaters and bird-watchers and sightseers. Madeline would be gone long before then.

She imagined Riley talking to his mother. He was probably mentioning the presumed association with Madeline right now.

She hadn't had to explain herself out of a predicament in years. No matter how she'd been as a child, she'd changed. She wasn't in pigtails anymore, and Riley would never be satisfied with thin excuses.

The quiet crunch of footsteps on the gravel path

let her know she didn't have much time to decide how best to explain.

He stopped at the railing a few feet away. Trying to gage his reaction, she studied his profile.

Nerves knotted her stomach. "Riley, there's something I need to tell you."

"I already know."

Chapter Six

It was just as Madeline had suspected. Riley was aware that there was some sort of duplicity here.

She swallowed.

This was it, the moment of truth. "There's something I need to tell you about Aaron—"

"I don't want to hear about Aaron."

That didn't sound good at all.

"I saw you crying for him today," he said. "I get it. You'll always love him."

Madeline didn't know what that had to do with his mother's phone call.

"Look," he said. "Your fiancé's life was cut tragically short, but he was lucky to have been loved by a woman like you, to be mourned by a woman like you."

"Riley, Aaron—"

"This has nothing to do with your Aaron. And everything to do with this."

He swung her around and caught her gasp of surprise in his kiss. Her heart jolted, but he didn't wait for her to adjust to the thrust of his tongue. This time he took, her anguish, her heartache and her sigh. It was the most intimate of kisses, and it sent the pit of her stomach into a wild swirl. She moaned instinctively and tipped her head back, opening for him, softening for him, touching his tongue with hers.

It wasn't a kiss to be analyzed. It was a kiss to be experienced. A mating of heat and instinct, it obscured every thought except one.

More.

She wanted more, more of him, more of this. She wanted to fit her body so tightly to his she couldn't tell where she ended and he began. She wanted, for just a little while, to feel good, to feel happy, and to know he felt the same way.

She wound her arms around his neck, her back arched, her fingers splaying wide through his soft wavy hair. His hands kneaded her back, urgent and exploratory, molding her to the length of him. He moaned, too, the sound of it touching her like some unforeseen knowledge that held the answers to questions she hadn't asked yet.

They drew apart slowly, arms, lips and breaths. When she opened her eyes, she saw that his were still half-hooded. A vein pulsed in his neck and his breathing was ragged. He was as dazed as she.

"See what I mean?" he said.

She could only shake her head. He was making a point. But what point?

"Riley," she said, trying again, "Aaron—"

This time he placed his fingertip to her lips. "Forgive me for being blunt, but he's dead, Madeline. You're alive, and you're allowed, no, you're *entitled* to feel it. And so am I."

He didn't know.

The realization ran through her mind twice before she grasped it. It was the only possible explanation.

He didn't know.

Perhaps he hadn't taken his mother's call. Or perhaps they hadn't talked about her. Either way, he didn't know she hadn't come to Gale to take his pulse for his mother.

Madeline was back to square one, uncertain how to proceed. "It's time we were getting back," she said.

Riley could have used another minute or two out in the cool air. He'd always heard a man's sex drive peaked at seventeen. A fat lot the experts knew. He was thirty-two and he felt as rangy and ready as he had at seventeen, only better because he knew a hell of a lot more about sex now.

He hadn't planned that last kiss. It had been a male reflex, a caveman staking his claim. He was no saint. Hell, he'd done what any man would do to temporarily wipe another man's image from a woman's mind, a woman he had every intention of having in his bed.

If he hadn't happened to look through the windshield at Madeline, he would have answered his phone. Instead he'd sat perfectly still, mesmerized by the way the breeze had played with her hair and pressed her shirt against her body, delineating the shape of her breasts. He'd wanted to peel it over her head, to take her breasts into his hands, to bend down to place a kiss on each one, to lay her down and take her then and there.

By the time he'd gotten his breathing under control, his mother had left a voice mail message. He'd listened to it then hurriedly dashed off a text message.

Doing well, Mom. In the middle of something. Will call soon. R.

No, he hadn't planned to kiss Madeline, but what a kiss. Now she was wrapping her arms around herself again, retreating. Her eyes were round and blue and filled with emotions she couldn't contain.

He walked her to the car and opened the passenger door for her. Whether she realized it or not, it was symbolic.

It was Riley's turn to drive.

It wasn't late when Madeline walked into Sully's Pub alone.

She hadn't lost track of time during the drive back to Gale. Quite the contrary, she'd felt the passing of every second.

Cigarette smoke curled at the low ceiling. The juke box blared from the back of the room, competing with the baseball game droning from the television over the bar. The pub wasn't crowded on this Sunday evening. Sissy was waitressing again. The bartender was a younger version of the man who'd served up margaritas Friday night.

Despite the noise, Madeline could hear Ruby O'Toole yelling for her to join her at the pool table. She finished giving Sissy her pizza order, then strode back to say hello.

She recognized Todd and Amanda from the other night, and Ruby introduced her to two other men who were with their small group around the pool table. The first was her brother, Connor, the other his friend Jason Horning. For some reason that name sounded familiar.

Connor O'Toole was tall, his hair a dark chestnut-brown. Jason was shorter, and had black hair and a goatee. Madeline stood between them, watching as Ruby missed an easy shot.

When it was the opponents' turn, Ruby slipped around behind Madeline and quietly said, "I'll keep an eye on the door for you. So far I don't see him."

Madeline spun around. Was she that transparent?

Evidently she was, for the striking redhead winked at her. "I take it Riley will be joining you?"

Madeline blinked in surprise. He'd gone to his house to let the dog out. She expected him back any minute. "How did you know?"

"Girlfriend, those are stars in your eyes."

Before Madeline could dispute it, she heard a stir at the front of the room. She turned around, fully expecting to see Riley. Instead a tall, muscular man with a nearly shaved head stood at the end of the bar.

Ruby's mouth fell open the way Madeline's often did. The song on the jukebox ended. Somebody turned down the volume on the TV. Through the ensuing silence, the young bartender said, "Trust me, pal, you don't want to be here."

"Hey, Ruby," the man said.

The color drained out of Ruby's face. "What are you doing here, Peter?" she asked, walking toward him.

Peter? As in Cheater Peter? Madeline thought. Uh-oh.

"Sully's is mine," Ruby said. "You get The Alibi. Fitting, isn't it?"

The man looked around as if gauging the crowd. He had the physique of a body builder and towered over the other men in the room. "Aw, Rube. How many times can I say I'm sorry? How many ways?"

"I want you to leave." Ruby sounded miserable.

"I can't eat. I can't sleep," he said huskily. "You're all I can think about."

"You weren't thinking about me when you were with that tramp Desiree."

Somewhere a woman said, "Good one, Ruby."

And a man said, "Did she say Desiree?"

Peter had the sense to grimace. "I'm sorry. I mean it, Ruby. I am. I swear, it'll never happen again."

"If you don't get out of my sight, *I* swear, I'll find Garret's olive fork behind the bar and—"

"All right, I'm going, but I love you and I'm not giving up." He cast one last beseeching look at her then walked out, closing the door just short of a slam.

In the ensuing silence, Riley walked in.

He stood for a moment in that stance Madeline had come to associate with him alone, shoulders straight, hands on his hips, feet apart. While everyone was still watching, his gaze found hers.

Madeline's heartbeat quickened. How could she feel such joy upon seeing him when she'd only known him for two days, when she was still aching for Aaron, when she had no business feeling this way?

Beside her Jason Horning said, "She'll probably take the jerk back." He was talking to Connor, but looking at Ruby.

Suddenly Madeline remembered why his name sounded familiar. This was the man who would walk across hot coals for Ruby. Ruby's brother, Connor, was looking at Sissy the same way. Sissy glanced at the young bartender, who suddenly developed a keen interest in the baseball game on TV.

Madeline wondered about the elements at work here. Jason wanted Ruby. Ruby didn't know what she wanted. Ruby's brother, Connor, was interested in Sissy. Apparently Sissy had unfinished business with the young bartender.

And what about her and Riley? she thought.

As if in answer, he strode directly to her and kissed her cheek. The touch of his lips on her skin felt like one of those childhood wishes to go back and do something over, only better, because she knew something now that she hadn't known then.

"Hey, Riley," one of the men at the bar said. "Was that your poster I saw on the light pole on the corner?"

Riley barely spared a glance at the man.

Madeline was mesmerized by the warmth in his

gaze. Scientists around the world were theorizing that something profound was taking place in the stratosphere. It was affecting rain forests and the oceans' tides, weather patterns and the effects of the sun. Whatever was happening, it surpassed the physical and was affecting behaviors and relationships everywhere on the globe.

The people in this small bar could have attested to that.

"If nobody claims him, you should name him Midas," the man who'd brought it up stated, obviously oblivious to the undercurrents swirling among half the people in the room.

"I think he looks like a Chief," someone else said.

"Duke."

"Mr. Howl."

"Mr. Howl? Please. He's a Sarge if I ever saw one."

Madeline and Riley stood a foot apart, connected by a force as powerful as nature itself, in harmony no matter what the orbiting moon had to do with it. "Comet," she said.

She was thinking about shooting stars.

"Didn't I tell you the new veterinarian would ask you out, Summer?" Madeline looked out the window as she shifted the cell phone against her ear.

It was one of those ink-black nights that made the

stars seem like tiny pinpricks in black velvet. The moon was a narrow sliver, and the mercury lights dotting the shore were surrounded by soft blue halos.

"His name is Jake Nichols," Summer said as if bored with the topic.

Summer Matthews dated now and then, but she always kept things light. Madeline was one of the few people who knew why.

"I'd be willing to bet your date tonight was far more eventful than mine," Summer said.

Startled out of her reverie, Madeline watched the yellow lights of a ship glide by. "I didn't have a date tonight."

"Uh-huh. Has Riley named his dog yet?"

"He still won't admit it's his dog."

Settling on one end of the sofa in the small cottage, Madeline curled her legs underneath her. In a chatty mood, she recounted the story of how Riley had put up posters around town. She told Summer about Fiona, too, and Ruby and Cheater Peter and the waitress, Sissy, and the bartender—Madeline couldn't remember his name—and everything that had happened at Sully's Pub while she was waiting for her pizza to bake.

"Was Riley there, too?" Summer asked.

Madeline nodded even though Summer couldn't see.

She and Riley hadn't stayed at Sully's long.

They'd picked up the pizza when it was ready, and ate it in his car in her driveway like a couple of teenagers on a Friday night.

"He hired a truck and movers to cart out all the furniture he's finally taken a look at and doesn't like. They start tomorrow."

"But you're not seeing him," Summer said.

"There's seeing someone and there's *seeing* someone," Madeline explained.

"Did he pick you up tonight?"

"I drove his Porsche."

"A Porsche, really?" And then, "Did he bring you home?"

"He lives right next door."

"Did he kiss you good-night?"

Madeline's fingertips went to her lips. He'd kissed her in the front seat of his car with the pizza box between them, on the sidewalk beneath the slivered moon and at her door in the shadow of the cottage. She should have been weak in the knees, and yet she felt stronger than she had in a very long time.

She sighed over the phone.

"That's what I thought," Summer said affectionately. "You're seeing Riley Merrick, all right."

Madeline sighed again, because Summer didn't know the half of it. If she wasn't careful, she could fall in love with him.

* * *

Madeline raised her fist to knock on Riley's door.

Noticing it shaking, she wrapped her other hand around it and looked around. It was the kind of balmy spring night Midwesterners waited all winter for, the kind that said, "There, see? Doesn't spring always come?"

For Madeline, it had been a long, sunless winter. Eighteen months, one week, and two days long to be exact. In some ways she felt like a coma patient, stiff from laying for so long, not quite certain how to start living again, but ready to feel the grass beneath her feet and the sun in her hair.

After her phone conversation with Summer, she'd stood for a long time in the shower. She'd lathered the cigarette smoke from Sully's out of her hair and scrubbed every inch of her skin. The sense that she needed to tell Riley the truth about his heart didn't wash away with hot water.

She wanted to tell him.

She had to tell him.

Her conviction grew stronger as she dried her hair. It followed her to the closet as she decided what to wear.

It was ten o'clock. Hoping it wasn't too late for an unannounced visitor, she knocked, surprised when the door opened an inch, and then two.

She poked her head inside. "Riley?"

The light was on in the kitchen and the dog was sprawled out on his pillow on the other side of the room. He opened one eye. Seeing it was only her, he closed it again and commenced to snore.

"Some watchdog you are," she said affectionately, and then, a little louder, "Hello? Anybody home?"

Riley's car was in the driveway, lights were on all through the house, and the door was unlocked. Surely he was here somewhere.

She tried the dining room next. Blueprints were spread across the table she'd uncovered earlier that afternoon and a chair was pulled out, as if he'd been sitting in it and had only just now gotten up.

"Riley?"

She continued on into the living room where the orange-and-green sofa looked so glaringly out of place even amidst all the clutter. Although there was still no sign of Riley, she could hear a television. The only TV she'd seen had been on the wall in the master bedroom.

And she wasn't going in there.

"Riley?" she called from the doorway that led down the hall. From here she could see the prescription bottles lined up neatly on the counter in the bathroom. Inside were the pills he took to keep from rejecting his new heart.

Her own heart thudded. For the first time since Aaron's accident, she felt as if something beautiful truly had come from something wrenchingly tragic.

"Riley?" Two of the doorways were dark, but light spilled from the master bedroom at the end of the narrow hall.

She'd gone as far as she could go and was turning around to leave when she heard something. It sounded like the quiet thud of a door, followed by footsteps.

She saw Riley a heartbeat before he saw her. He stood at the end of the hallway wearing nothing but a towel. Fresh from a shower, his hair looked almost black. Water droplets clung to his chest, glistening white on the long scar down its center.

As he stood there looking back at her, his towel slowly slid from his hips. He stepped over it, the action drawing her eyes lower. Not that she could have kept her gaze from going there.

"I was just thinking about you," he said without an ounce of self-consciousness. "Who says wishes don't come true."

He held out his hand, bidding her to come closer.

Feeling her face flame and her mouth go slack, she spun around and did the only rational thing she could think to do. She ran, past the orange-and-green sofa, past the dining room table and the sleeping dog. She ran, out the door, across the lawn and through the gap in the arborvitae hedge.

But she didn't outrun the memory of Riley Merrick, fully aroused.

Riley found Madeline sitting in the dark in an old Adirondack chair behind the cottage. He'd thrown on some clothes before walking over, but as far as he knew, she hadn't looked at him. Since he hadn't tried to be quiet, she had to have heard him approach. He didn't ask if he could sit down. Instead, he stopped directly in front of her chair.

"I'm a little surprised to see you so soon," she said.

Her hands went to either side of her face. The narrow sliver of moonlight was too weak to reach all the way to the earth's surface, therefore he couldn't actually see the blush on her cheeks. He smiled because she was so adorably innocent. "It isn't as if you've never seen a naked man."

She turned her head in surprise. And it dawned on him that she was awfully innocent for a modern woman, for any modern woman, but especially for a woman who'd been engaged.

"Madeline?" he said, taking her hand.

She looked up at him looking down at her. She remained seated and he continued to hold her hand, his thumb drawing half circles on her cool skin.

"I've never. Um. That is, I was saving, er, it, for my wedding night."

He was pretty sure he'd known a virgin or two in his lifetime. He was positive he'd never taken one to bed. He would have known, and he would have remembered.

She held perfectly still, as if waiting to see what he would do with her admission.

"The only thing this changes," he said, his voice husky in his own ears, "is the way I'll make love to you the first time."

Madeline felt herself being drawn to her feet. And then Riley was framing her face with both his hands, sliding his fingers over her cheekbones, over the delicate curves of her ears. Even in the black pearl darkness she could see the possessive gleam in his eyes.

She raised a palm to his cheek. With one fingertip she touched the groove beside his mouth then slowly glided her fingernail over his lips. She knew an enormous power when the groove deepened, when he moaned into her hand.

He slipped his fingers into her hair, anchoring her face for his kiss. At the onset, the touch of his mouth on hers felt like a solemn promise to protect her, to hold what was dear. Her eyes fluttered closed, and his passion rose.

Her answering response shouldn't have been shocking, but a shock ran through her nonetheless. She backed up so quickly and with so much vehemence the backs of her legs bumped the edge of the chair.

She could tell it cost him to let her go.

"I'll never pressure you, Madeline," he said. And she knew it was another promise. "I'll leave the door unlocked. The light will be on when you're ready. I'll be waiting."

She lost sight of him in the darkness and had to rely on sound to chart his progress across the narrow yard and through the gap in the arborvitae hedge. She must have imagined the click of his back door opening and closing, for the house was too far away to hear that, but in her mind's eye she saw him standing in his kitchen.

She looked out across the water then up at the dark sky before opening the cottage's back door. She went in, then stood leaning against the door, her heart beating and her mind reeling. Panicking, she took a step in one direction, then another, only to stop each time.

She was unable to flee, unable to even pace. All she could do was stand in the quiet in the dark, her breathing deep and shallow by turns. Her bra felt restrictive suddenly, her skirt heavy on her hips.

Her body knew exactly what she wanted.

She wanted Riley's hands on her skin. She wanted it so badly she half expected to be able to beam herself there with a blink of her eye.

Oh, that life could be that easy.

After Aaron died, she hadn't been able to take pleasure in anything without feeling guilty. There wasn't even joy in the simple things like eating and sleeping and working. She'd been enjoying nearly every moment since she'd set foot in Gale. Although it made her ache, it was more like the feeling she had while watching the horizon swell into sunrise, as if the human body had no capacity to process such incredible beauty.

He said he would leave the door open and the light on. He'd said he would be waiting.

The next step was up to her. If she dared.

Chapter Seven

Riley was at the sink when he heard a sound at his back door. Madeline walked in, the bravest woman he'd ever known, and stood taking him in. The long sleeves of her shirt were pushed up, the result of a bout of nerves, most likely. The top two buttons were open, allowing him a glimpse of skin he was going to take his time exploring. Her skirt skimmed her body like a whisper. It was casual, sexy as hell.

"You're taking a chance leaving your door unlocked that way you know," she said. "Anybody could have gotten in."

"I didn't leave it unlocked for just anyone."

There went the pit of Madeline's stomach again. She didn't know how Riley could be so calm when she was a bundle of nerves. She didn't think she'd ever seen a more appealing man than him standing at a sink full of dishes, his feet bare, a towel slung over one shoulder, his shirt hanging open to reveal his washboard stomach and a little higher, his scar.

Men and women were so different, even when it came to sex. And no matter how she sugarcoated this, that's what this was.

She'd taken the shortcut through the gap in the arborvitae hedge, knowing full well that every step brought her closer to Riley and her first time. She couldn't believe she was really here. She only knew that if she hadn't come over, she would have regretted it for the rest of her life.

He put down the dish he'd been drying and dropped the towel on top of it. When he took a step toward her, she took a step, too. They met in the middle of the room, her heart pounding as if she'd been running.

"I wasn't sure you'd come," he said.

She considered the dimmed lights and the soft music and his unbuttoned shirt, and said, "You look pretty sure to me."

"Let's just say I was hoping." His smile did something to the pit of her stomach.

She knew what was on his mind. It was in the way

he moved, all animal prowess and masculine intent. It was in his scent, a hint of aftershave and something that was uniquely him. It was in the way he twined his fingers with hers. He wasn't rushing her; his patience enveloped her in warmth. For the first time in a long time there were no shadows across her heart. He was giving her time, and it was such a gift, this shared moment.

As he started toward the dining room, she went with him, her steps matching his. She was only vaguely aware of the rooms as they passed, for suddenly they were in his bedroom. His arms came around her, drawing her against the hard length of him. His breathing deepened. Hers hitched.

She'd expected his arousal, and yet the feel of it against her belly through their clothes made her go momentarily still. Sensing her nerves, he held her more gently, surprising her with how attuned he was to what she was feeling. And she knew she had nothing to fear from him.

In the absence of fear, need took over, a man's need for a woman, and a woman's need for a man. When it seemed he would never stop kissing her mouth, his lips trailed down her neck, nuzzling the sensitive skin at the base of her throat. He unbuttoned her sweater and dragged it down her arms, turning it inside out in his haste, letting it fall where it may.

And then his eyes were on the swells of her breasts in her lacy bra. She reached behind her back, her fingers on the closure, but he stilled her fingertips with his own.

"Easy," he said. "We're going to take this one step at a time."

His voice was husky, his brown eyes heavy-lidded and filled with everything it was going to cost him to do things that way. The zipper down the back of her skirt rasped as he lowered it. With a gentle sway of her hips, the skirt fell to the floor and swished around her feet. She stepped over it, back into his arms.

One moment they were standing, her bare thighs against his jean-clad knees, and the next he was slowly lowering her to the bed, and the mattress was shifting at her back and he was easing down next to her. She turned onto her side, facing him, soft where he was hard, smooth where he wasn't.

He ran his hand along the length of her body, massaging her neck, kneading her shoulder, gliding along her waist, her hip, her thigh. As he discovered the things she liked, and the things she loved, he nuzzled her neck with his lips, pressed a kiss along the edge of her jaw, and finally on her mouth once again.

His fingers worked through her hair, slowly gliding along the outside of her neck, spreading wide at the base of her throat, his palm resting for a moment over her heart. She'd had no idea a simple touch could cause her heart to speed up so, sending desire pulsing through her. Coherent thoughts were replaced with sensations, the flutter of awareness, the thrill of desire and the yearning to know him as she'd never known another man, to feel his weight on her, his breath blending with her breath, their hearts beating as one.

She rolled onto her back, reveling in the large mattress beneath her and the tall man straddling her. She may have been a virgin, but she wasn't completely naive. She reached between their bodies, and covered him with her hand. His jeans came off as if she'd said, "Abracadabra." Her bra and panties soon followed.

When Madeline was finally naked, Riley's breath caught. Why had he thought he preferred chesty women? Her breasts were firm and round and perfect, the centers pale brown, puckered and wet from his kiss. Her belly was flat, her naval a slight indentation he wanted to explore further. Her thighs were supple, her legs long and smooth.

In another part of the house, a CD ended and another began. Here in his bedroom there was the slight creak of the mattress shifting beneath them and the deep breaths they took. Trying desperately to slow this down, he traded places with her, him on his back, her sprawled on top of him. He wanted to be careful. He intended to be careful. She let him know what she thought of his best intentions, moving against him, skimming her hands over his heated skin, seeking, touching.

Everything he thought he knew about virgins was refuted by the way she kissed him, both giving and demanding. He reached between their bodies, and finally touched the part of her no man had taken. She rose against his hand and cried out.

The blinds were drawn against the night, so the light Riley saw had to be coming from another source of energy. It was the energy they were creating together, a kind of dawnlike aura that heated him from the inside. Crushing her to him, he pressed his mouth to hers. He forgot to breathe, but it didn't matter. His body didn't seem to require oxygen. He needed something far more vital than air.

He was holding on by a thread. He reached out to the nightstand and opened the foil packet with his teeth.

Levering his weight on one elbow, he held her gaze as he eased her legs a little farther apart. He'd never realized what a gift a woman could be. It was no wonder some cultures believed virgins were the ultimate reward, the pie in the sky, the promised pot of gold at the end of the rainbow waiting in the after-life for the faithful.

"Now, Riley," she whispered, her lips wet against his ear.

He did what she'd asked and what he couldn't have kept from doing if trumpets were blaring and the end of the world were imminent. He pressed deeper, watching her eyes as she accepted him an inch at a time. As he felt that last barrier give way, he began to move.

He lost track of time, but felt her shudder, gloried in it. He could no longer hold back. He willed himself to be gentle, but he couldn't contain his urgency. She cried out lustily, suddenly as insatiable as he was. The pleasure he felt in that moment was pure and wild. She cried out his name again. And everything exploded in a whirl of sensation. And after his own powerful release overtook him, he knew that one virgin was heaven enough for him.

Madeline was on her back in Riley's king-size bed, the sheet pulled all the way up to her neck. She could hear water running. Riley was in the adjoining bathroom, drawing her a bath. It was poignantly thoughtful of him, and brought fresh tears to her eyes. She hadn't expected to be so emotional after, well, afterward, for there had been weeping. And blood.

She wanted to burrow under the covers and hide until morning. For heaven's sakes, she'd just shared her body with him in the most intimate manner imaginable. Why this sudden bout of shyness?

Back from the bathroom, he lowered to the edge of the bed and smiled at her. "You okay?"

She nodded and did her best to appear calm and collected.

"Your bath is ready whenever you are," he said.

She could see the marks her fingernails had made on his back. She'd had no idea she would be such a wild woman in bed, or so noisy or responsive.

Where was a hidey hole when she needed one? Since asking him to turn his back would be embarrassing in itself, she decided to make do with speed and agility. She slid naked out of bed and slipped into the bathroom as quickly as she could.

He followed without an ounce of pretense, as naked as she. Wetting a washcloth with warm water, he handed it to her and kissed her gently before leaving the room, granting her the privacy she sought.

When she was ready, she looked at her surroundings. What a bathroom! The lights were dimmed, the stone tiles beautiful, the floor warm beneath her feet. Through the skylight over the oval tub she saw the light of one tiny star.

She couldn't find any bubble bath, so she drizzled shampoo beneath the waterspout. With steam rising and bubbles forming, she lowered into the large tub, the warm water working wonders on her most tender places. Settling back, she looked up at that lone star. She stretched her legs, pointed her toes, and closed her eyes for a moment.

The water was still running and steam was still rising when Riley's knock sounded on the door. He had two bottles of water in one hand and a small plate in the other. Being careful to stay under the bubbles, she held out her hand, accepting one of the bottles he offered.

While she took small sips, he tipped his bottle back, draining the entire contents. Wiping his mouth on the back of his hand, he said, "I brought cheese, too, but I couldn't find any crackers."

"This is fine," she said, her gaze traveling from his washboard stomach to his bony feet. She wondered if he often walked around completely naked.

"You're sure you don't want anything else?" he asked.

Meeting his gaze once more, she said, "I'd like to do that again."

He joined her in the bathtub so fast water sloshed over the side. Pulling her onto his lap, he said, "I was hoping you'd say that."

She caught her lower lip between her teeth to keep from smiling and said, "I could tell."

He chuckled, his hands already gliding over her soap-slick skin. His laugh trailed away, replaced by other sounds, sensual sounds she was learning by heart.

By the time they climbed out of the bathtub, the water was no longer steaming and the bubbles were all gone. Madeline's shyness had dissolved with them.

Riley's hand tingled; his arm was asleep, but he wasn't about to move it. He liked Madeline right where she was.

It was late, and the lights were low. She was curled on her side, her head on his shoulder, her knee nuzzling his thigh as she drew figure-eight patterns on his chest.

After their swim in his bathtub, he'd pulled on his jeans and she'd slipped into his shirt for a raid on his refrigerator. He'd made them an egg-and-cheese omelet, without nearly burning the house down this time. When they'd left the kitchen, they'd intended to take their hot midnight snack to bed. On the way through the living room she'd turned to him. They didn't make it back to the bedroom for a long time, ending up on that orange-and-green sofa in the living room. Eventually they'd picked up their plates again, and had devoured the lukewarm omelets and cold toast in the middle of the bed.

Their empty plates were on the nightstand now, their clothes on the floor again, and Madeline was snuggled up against him. "I'll never be able to look at a bathtub like yours without remembering that second time," she said sleepily. It was the closest either of them had come to alluding to the fact that their time together was temporary.

"Want to hear something ironic?" he asked. "That green-and-orange sofa is growing on me."

She smiled drowsily. "They say the third time's the charm. What do they say about the fourth time?"

His arms tightened around her, and hers wound around his neck, the soft contours of her body gliding across the harder surfaces of his. They moved over the bed, arms and legs entwined, lips clinging, hands seeking, giving pleasure and receiving it. She was crushed under him one moment, sprawled on top of him the next. But it wasn't enough. Touching, kissing, straining toward one another was only the beginning. What followed was a breathtaking roller coaster ride straight to the top. The finale was a free-fall bursting of sensation that blew every thought he'd ever had about lovemaking to smithereens.

His new heart was getting a hell of a workout.

Every so often, Madeline's eyes drifted closed. So this was sex, she thought, her head on Riley's shoulder again, her hair fanned out on the pillow beside her. This was passion.

She and Aaron had had several close calls over the years, but waiting had become a way of life. It was only until they finished high school, they'd promised, only until after college. Once they were engaged, it was only for a little longer. He died a month before they were to have said, "I do."

Since that horrible day, she'd imagined she would become one of those old women who kept a cat and wore lace collars and joined groups that made blankets for the needy. She'd imagined she would grow to enjoy her quiet existence. Now that she'd experienced passion, she didn't know how she was going to live without it for the rest of her life. Telling herself not to think about that now, she kissed Riley's shoulder then ran her fingertip down the scar. Finally she rested her palm over the center of his chest and sighed contentedly.

"What does it feel like?" he asked.

"Steady and strong," she said, planting a kiss at the edge of his scar. Something about the question made her rise up on one elbow and look at him. "Why did you ask?" When he said nothing, she said, "Riley, why?"

He shrugged. "I was just wondering."

For once she didn't let her mouth go slack. She

sensed she was getting to the bottom of something important and couldn't let this go. "Why would you have to wonder?"

"Forget it."

"Are you saying you can't feel your heart?" she asked.

She could tell he wished he hadn't brought it up, but he finally nodded. Outside the wind crooned. Inside there was only her gasp of dismay.

She eased a little farther away from him so she could see his face more clearly. His eyes were only half-open, his jaw covered with the shadow of a dark beard. Beneath her hand, his heart rate quickened.

Questions raced through her mind. Why could she feel it if he couldn't? What could have caused this condition? What was being done for it, for him? In the end, she asked, "Do the doctors know why?"

"Not really." He punched his pillows and settled back, the sheet around his waist, his hands behind his head. By now she knew him well enough to know that if she waited, he would continue.

He glanced at the ceiling, and then into her eyes. "The transplant went off like clockwork, my recovery one for the record books. According to the specialists, I'm a resounding success. The pills I swallow every day keep my body from attacking the new heart. There's only one little problem. I can't feel it beating. Did you know that a viable heart only lasts six hours? There's never enough time to do a cross match, and yet this heart settled into my chest as if it belonged there. Hell, it's as if it wants to be here. At first I wondered if it's so damned perfect, why couldn't I feel it? Now I don't think about it much."

Madeline's own heart beat ominously.

He laid his hand over hers on his chest. "I can feel it on my palm. I can even feel it through your hand. But I can't feel it inside my chest, not when I run, not even that second time in the bathtub."

"What do your doctors say?" she asked quietly.

"They hooked me up to a machine and blasted the heartbeat over loudspeakers. It sounded like a wild mustang galloping on solid ground. The specialists ruled out nerve damage and side effects to my medication. There's no physical explanation for the fact that I can't feel it."

She shivered suddenly, for she'd read of rare instances in which people who'd witnessed horrors on the battlefield or a grotesque crime stopped seeing the color red. She'd never heard of anyone unable to feel his own beating heart.

"What about a psychological explanation?" she whispered.

He drew the spread up around her shoulders and

made a sound that told her what he thought of the psychological evaluation. "The panel of psychiatrists I saw were keenly interested in how I feel about my mother, my father, my brothers and stepmothers, even the family dogs. I told them all the same thing. I have no idea why my chest feels like a cold slab of concrete, but I'm damn sure it doesn't have anything to do with my meddling mother, my dead father or the family Pekingeses. The profession as a whole needs to get new material."

This past year and a half Madeline had been so haunted by her loss she hadn't considered the possibility that Riley was going through his own kind of hell. How small-minded people became when they were in pain. Now she realized she wasn't the only one who'd suffered. Riley didn't tell her how sick he'd been prior to the transplant, but surely he'd have been dangerously close to death himself to have been put at the top of the transplant list at such a young age. While she and Aaron's parents had been keeping vigil in his hospital room that agonizing day, Riley and his family had been keeping another kind of vigil.

She wanted to ask what had happened, how he'd gotten so ill, and if he'd been afraid of dying. Since she couldn't voice any of those questions, she pressed her hand to his chest. Her heart brimming with tenderness, she said, "I'm so sorry you can't feel this."

"Try lower."

He could still surprise her. And she could still blush, but she glided her hand down his rib cage. "You are so wicked," she whispered.

She spread her fingers wide across his washboard stomach, eased past his naval, a little wicked herself. When she found him, he let out a sound of pleasure.

The next thing she knew, they were rolling across his bed, and he was kissing a trail of his own. He got a little sidetracked with her breasts. She loved it when he kissed her there, when he suckled, laving each in turn with his tongue, for it sent sensations to places in her body physically unconnected.

Every time they made love she learned something new, about him, and about herself. Every time she thought sex couldn't get any better. And every time she was wrong.

As the sky outside the window was just beginning to lighten, she thought about all she'd discovered since meeting Riley. She'd recalled things about her own personality she'd buried. Throughout the process of remembering, some of those traits and characteristics had slowly begun to emerge once again.

Completely on her own for the first time in her life here in Gale, she'd taken risks. She'd broken a few rules, maybe more than a few, had a few drinks and discovered that she could still laugh. She'd made a few wonderful new friends and shed new tears. She'd found a part of herself she'd forgotten and discovered a part she hadn't known existed until now. And in the process, she'd fallen in love again, with the last person she was ever supposed to have met.

She'd come to Gale to prove to herself that Riley Merrick was alive and well. And she was the one coming back to life.

Chapter Eight

It was morning. And it was Monday. That was the extent of Madeline's cognitive skills, at least until she managed to pry her eyes open. That wasn't entirely true, she thought, smiling to herself. It was a wonderful Monday morning. She knew that with her eyes closed.

Squinting against the bright sunlight slanting through the narrow slats in the blinds, she sat up. The other side of the bed was empty. Unfamiliar with the protocol for mornings after, she padded to the bathroom where she splashed her face with warm water and finger-combed her impossibly mussed hair. She wished she'd have thought to bring a toothbrush, but made do with a dab of toothpaste on the end of her finger. After donning her clothes and straightening them as best she could, she went looking for Riley.

She found him on the phone in the dining room. His back to her, he leaned over blueprints spread across the table. He was fully dressed in dark chinos and a blue knit shirt.

"There isn't enough support in the attic floor joists to sustain a fireplace that massive." He listened, shook his head. "We found them the Riker and we're putting a glass floor in the foyer. They didn't want a second story, they wanted vaulted ceilings and enormous open rooms and five bathrooms and a home theater and a gym."

He shook his head again. "I understand that, Kipp, and I support their vision, but unfortunately that ceiling won't. How would they get to the second floor? A staircase would completely block the view of the lake. Did you explain that to them?" He looked more closely at the blueprint. "You and I both know we can do it. We also both know it would entail major design changes, and those are costly and time-prohibitive." He listened for a few more moments, mumbled something Madeline didn't hear then flipped the phone closed.

"Trouble?" she asked.

He turned at the sound of her voice and gave her

a smile that put her in mind of long kisses and late nights. "Nothing out of the ordinary," he said.

She sauntered closer. "Have you been up long?"

"Twenty minutes, maybe. The coffee should be ready by now."

His hair waved over the tops of his ears, a little too long to be considered civilized. Folding down his collar, she said, "I'm not sure I'm good for you. When I arrived on Friday, you were an early riser, clean-shaven and unwrinkled."

"Believe me, you're good for me." Riley's grip tightened possessively on her upper arm. He should have been exhausted. At the very least, he should have been sated. Instead, he found he wanted her all over again.

He reminded himself that the clients were flying in. So, with great reluctance, he let his hand fall to his side.

Felix and Gabriella Braxton's newest movie had premiered at a film festival in Chicago over the weekend. As long as they were so close, they were going to hop aboard their airplane and take a look at the progress Merrick and Dawson Enterprises was making on their lake house. Riley and Kipp needed to come up with a preliminary solution to their newest demands before they arrived.

Watching Madeline pour coffee into a mug in the kitchen, he said, "For some reason, I don't want to go to work today. Any idea why that might be?"

She took a sip before handing the cup to him. Filling another for herself, she said, "If memory serves me correctly, I can think of several."

That attitude, he thought, that all-knowing, sexy as hell grin. He wanted to sample it, all of it, all of her, from her provocative smile to her warm, pliant body. Making a sound of frustration, he said, "You're only here until Friday. I hate to waste a minute of it at work."

Madeline averted her face to hide an instant squeezing hurt. She couldn't fault Riley for reminding her that this was temporary. He'd laid out his parameters from the beginning. Five days, he'd said.

She had no experience in flings. Yesterday Riley had said he didn't do forever well. Did anyone have forever, really? Perhaps all anyone could do was seize the moment and leave the future for another day.

"Late yesterday I arranged for a moving company to come today to cart off the furniture," Riley was saying. "I'll have to reschedule."

"You don't have to do that," she said, surprising both of them. "I can organize the movers."

"You don't mind?" he asked.

"Not at all. In fact, I'd enjoy it. Just tell me what you want to keep."

"Surprise me," he said from the dining room where he was gathering up blueprints.

"Wait," she said, getting between him and the back door. "I don't even know your taste."

His eyes were a deep, dark brown this morning, warm enough to slip into. "I've got to tell you, right now, my taste is leaning toward blue-eyed blondes. I'll be back as soon as I can."

He kissed her hard. A moment later he was gone.

Dazed, Madeline carried her coffee to the table. Tracing the now-familiar scorch marks with one finger, she wondered if it was too late to tell Riley about his heart. What could she say to make him believe that her reason for coming to Gale had been a sincere wish to see that something beautiful had come from something dreadful? How could she prove that she hadn't orchestrated any of this, from their first encounter at the construction site to last night in bed?

He'd left an imprint on her heart just as surely as he'd left one on the table, but she was afraid it was too late to try to explain. She hadn't planned to meet him any more than she'd planned to fall in love with him. She sighed, for even the goals she had set out to accomplish weren't going well. The dog still didn't have a name, and Riley couldn't feel his new heart.

Just then a loud knock rattled the front door. Moving a curtain aside, she saw a white moving van in the driveway. Riley had scheduled the movers. She supposed that was progress.

The dog got off his green pillow and looked at her in silent expectation. "All right," she said on the way to answer the door. "This morning, we'll oversee the movers. It'll be a labor of love for both of us, won't it?"

Felix and Gabriella Braxton didn't bring mayhem with them wherever they went. They produced it the same way they produced blockbuster movies, with incredible finesse, great brilliance and temper tantrums worthy of Oscar nominations.

Riley had picked the Braxtons up at the airstrip. He'd duly admired Felix's private plane and listened patiently to their latest dreams for their lake house. Now, the clients were in another area at Merric and Dawson headquarters, and Kipp was leafing through the sketches Riley had made, first one, then another, and another. Finally he threw the entire stack into the wastebasket next to Riley's desk.

"You're right," Kipp said. "That house was designed around that view, and every one of those new sketches blocks it in one way or another. There's no good place for a staircase in that great room."

Riley leaned back in his chair and shrugged at

his closest friend and business partner. The building that housed Merrick & Dawson Enterprises had
been a furniture factory in another incarnation.
Located on the outskirts of Traverse City, its wall
of windows overlooking the bay was completely
impractical six months out of the year. Clients
loved it. And clients were the reason they were in
business.

From the beginning Riley and Kipp had left the
cookie-cutter subdivisions with their fake dormers
and postage stamp lots to other developers. While
property that had once been deemed useless by anyone who wasn't a farmer or orchard grower was suddenly catching on like wildfire by developers, Riley
and Kipp had taken a risk, choosing to specialize in
one-of-a-kind houses. Fifteen years ago, real estate
was the new frontier. Resorts and gated communities
had sprung up from Chicago to Mackinaw City.
Now, with the economy in its greatest downturn in
nearly three-quarters of a century in every corner of
the country, developments sat half-finished, the exposed wood twisting and rotting in the elements.

These past few years, Riley and Kipp had altered
their strategy to include energy-efficient windows
and furnaces and green materials, and were busier
than ever. Because their building sites were often
well away from metropolises, they rarely had to deal

with city planning committees and annexation meetings. They did, however, have to cater to the whims of their decadently wealthy clients.

"Are you going to say something?" Kipp groused. "Or are you just going to sit there, looking like you've just climbed out of a woman's bed?"

Riley gave Kipp a rare smile.

With a dawning look of understanding, Kipp scratched his chin and said, "No wonder you're so mellow."

Actually, it was Riley's own bed he'd climbed out of, but he didn't kiss and tell.

"It's that blonde nurse, isn't it? I figured she'd be good for you."

Riley couldn't help thinking about the way Madeline had looked this morning, her blue eyes sleepy, her face pretty and pale, and her lips naturally pink and utterly kissable. Her clothes had been slightly disheveled, and the color the silver lining of a cloud. He was getting philosophical, for until he'd met her, he hadn't believed something as poetic as a cloud's silver lining existed.

Madeline Sullivan was five feet five inches tall, and a very nice five feet five, at that. She wore her clothes well. A lot of women were five-five and looked good in light-colored sweaters and skirts that rode low on their hips. Thoughts of them didn't flood into his mind when he was in the middle of a three-engine fire at work. Which meant it wasn't Madeline's hair or clothes that made it impossible to get her out of his head. It was the way he'd felt since she'd burst onto the job site on Friday.

Work had been his constant these past eighteen months. It was the one area of his life that hadn't changed. The business of designing and building incredible and unique houses kept him in form, kept him fit, kept him focused. Normally the challenge of unforeseen problems, consultations and solutions energized him. Today, he wanted to drive straight home, turn off his phone, draw the blinds and spend the day in bed. With Madeline.

"Well? Are you going to tell me about her?" Kipp prodded.

"No. Do you think you can handle this?" Riley asked. "Without me, I mean?"

Kipp steepled his fingers beneath his chin. The clients were with the company's resident designer. Arlene Straus knew wainscoting and scraped hickory floors, cultured stone, imported marble, solid granite, gourmet kitchens, lighting and fixtures better than any designer Kipp had ever met, including Riley's stepmother. Nobody pushed Arlene around. She'd just gotten back from getting a custom latte for Gabriella.

"Go on," Kipp said. "I can handle Felix and Gabbie."

"They're in the movie business," Riley said, finding his feet.

"Yes, I know."

"I've been thinking about this. Scenes in movies are shot out of sequence. Drive them out to their property and show them their lake house as if through a camera lens. Take them up on the plywood deck and stand where their great room is going to be and let them see the view of Lake Michigan and the dunes and the distant towns. If they still want a stairway in the middle of that, we'll give them a stairway. But watch your back. Gabriella is a groper."

"Yeah, I know. She caught me unawares half an hour ago practically right under her husband's nose."

Riley left, and an hour later, Kipp could hardly believe how easy it had been. Felix and Gabriella had not only embraced the idea of driving to their property, they'd considered it an adventure to climb a fifteen-foot ladder so they could stand in their new vacation home on the shores of a freshwater ocean and imagine where they would arrange their furniture to best utilize those views.

Leaving them to their discussion, Kipp wandered to the far end of the building and lit a cigarette. He tried not to wonder where he would be if his mother hadn't dumped him off at the Merrick Estate seventy-five miles south of here all those years ago. Riley treated him like a brother, but Kipp never forgot where he came from. From the beginning, Riley had had his back. Kipp would take a bullet for him. It had been a relief to see him looking almost happy this morning.

He felt his phone vibrate in his pocket. If anybody had been looking, they would have seen him smile as he said hello to Riley's mother. "No, he's gone for the day, Chloe." Kipp took a draw on his cigarette while he listened. "He was at the office earlier. Yes, I saw him with my own two eyes. I wouldn't lie to you. Riley's fine. Fit as a fiddle." Kipp grimaced, for Chloe Merrick could wring the truth out of him better than anybody he knew. "As far as I know, he was going home. He has plans, Chloe. I'm sure he's—"

Chloe didn't let him finish before saying goodbye and hanging up.

He instantly punched in Riley's number to give him a heads-up. It went directly to voice mail. Riley had already turned off his phone. Damn.

Kipp didn't hear Gabriella saunter up behind him. By the time he felt her pat him on the ass, it was too late. He'd jumped, and swore. "We need to put a bell on you," he said to the green-eyed movie director with the cute little body that belied her actual age.

"Sorry," she said.

"I'm just glad it wasn't your husband. That would have been awkward."

"You have a way about you," she said, intelligence in those green eyes. "You make flawed people feel accepted."

"And you make unsuspecting men nearly jump off buildings."

"We all have our gifts. Did Riley run off and leave you here all alone?" she asked.

"Something came up."

"A family emergency?"

Kipp thought about Chloe's phone call. "God I hope not," he said, and he meant every word.

"There, there. This isn't so bad, is it?"

Riley was almost past the bathroom off the hallway when he remembered he hadn't taken his pills this morning. He backtracked, dumped the proper dosage into his hand, and downed them all.

"See? It's better when you just relax and let it happen, isn't it?"

Medicine had never been easier to swallow. That might have had something to do with the mental picture Madeline was painting for him. He put the lids back on the bottles once again before following that voice, that sexy, crooning voice.

He found her in the master bathroom. At some point she'd gone back to the cottage and changed. She now wore blue jeans and if he wasn't mistaken, the T-shirt she'd bought at a gift shop in Charlevoix yesterday. She was bent over the tub, her hair wet in places, soggy towels beside her, water everywhere. In the middle of the bathtub sat one wet brown dog.

The dog turned beseeching eyes to Riley.

"Don't look at me," Riley said. "I can smell you from here."

Madeline glanced over her shoulder and saw Riley leaning in the doorway, one shoulder resting along the frame, arms and ankles crossed. "He rolled in a rotten fish. How do you like the house?"

"It looks good."

She was pleased he liked it. It had taken two men less than two hours to cart away the furniture. They'd even helped her arrange the pieces she'd instructed them to leave behind. It seemed to her that Riley had mentioned that one of his stepmothers was an interior decorator. Maybe one of these days he would ask her to finish decorating.

"You left the mahogany table in the kitchen," he said.

She nodded and lunged for the dog. She hadn't been able to bring herself to tell the movers to take the table that had sustained Riley through so many sleepless nights. "You're not tumbleweed. You're a tree."

"I guess that explains that."

She smiled to herself, but didn't elaborate. "Your dog doesn't like baths or men in white coveralls," she said as she finished lathering dog shampoo into the thick brown coat. "He parked himself in front of the door and growled—he growls as if he means it— every time the movers tried to come in. I finally had to ask them to take off their coveralls."

"You asked the movers to undress before coming in?"

"They were wearing clothes underneath." She took the handheld nozzle and began to rinse the soap suds down the drain. Of course the dog shook, spraying water everywhere.

Again.

Riley was there suddenly with two more towels. He had him towel dried in almost no time. With his fur sticking up all over, the dog walked stiff legged from the bathroom to sulk.

"And the orange-and-green sofa?" Riley asked, dropping the soggy towels into the bathtub. "I can't wait to hear your reason for leaving that in the living room."

She rose slowly, drying her arms. "After last night that has sentimental value. I hope you don't mind."

"Do I look like I mind?"

She smiled because he looked good. "Now I'm the one who needs a shower."

He reached around and turned on the water in the large, walk-in shower. "I can help with that."

He peeled her wet T-shirt over her head, turning it inside out in the process. She helped him out of his shirt, and they both did away with their pants. In almost no time they were both naked and she was gliding her hands up his chest, sliding her arms around his shoulders. At the same time, his arms went around her waist, bodily lifting her off her feet. She wrapped her legs around his waist, their mouths joined.

They moaned through openmouthed kisses, warm water pouring over them from above, getting in their eyes and bouncing off their shoulders, running down their backs, making their skin slick.

Her arms went around his neck, the action bringing her breasts close to his mouth. She was wanton, her long-dormant sexuality newly awakened to every sound, every touch, every sensation. She pressed closer to him, her ankles locked behind him, her breathing ragged, her eyes closed to the onslaught of rushing water, her heart open to the joy he brought her, her body open to the passion unfurling from him to her, and back again.

Madeline never knew she could make love without her feet ever touching the floor. It was hot, hard and fast. With steam curling from every direction, her heart was brimming and so full she wished this idyllic week never had to end.

Eventually they were going to have to rouse themselves out of bed and get something to eat. Madeline's hair had dried after that incredible shower an hour ago.

"Is this normal?" she asked.

"Is what normal?"

Her breast had come uncovered, and she caught him looking at it, already distracted. Smiling to herself because she secretly liked how easily she could distract him, she said, "This. Sex. Does the average person have sex, you know, so often?"

"This," he said, laving her exposed breast with his tongue, "is far above average, so far above average I'd call it magnificent." He moved to her other breast. "Supremely spectacular—superhuman, even."

She giggled, and it came out sounding wanton and breathless. "Braggart."

"I was talking about you."

It was all it took, and she was with him again, lips to lips, chest to breast, hip to hip, hearts beating, breaths ragged, hands seeking, bodies straining in that age-old rhythm that carried from the dawn of time.

"Ri-ley?"

He stopped, and held perfectly still.

"Yoo-hoo. Ri. Lee. Anybody home? Oh. When did you get a dog?"

Riley groaned. "Oh, no."

Madeline went still, too.

Whoever was in the house was getting steadily closer. "Did Gwen finally get in touch with you? I know she's been beside herself wanting to do something with this place."

"Who is that?" Madeline asked.

Riley would recognize that voice anywhere. "My mother has the worst timing in the world."

"Your mother?" If it was possible to shriek in a whisper, Madeline did exactly that.

They both jumped up. Riley grabbed his jeans. She dragged the sheet off the bed.

"I know you're here somewhere, dear. Your car's parked right outside. Kipp insists you're fine, but he's hiding something. I'm your mother, and believe me, a mother just knows. We sense these things."

Riley managed to get his pants partially zipped before his mother burst into his bedroom. She smiled at him and was on her way over to plant a motherly kiss on his cheek when she noticed Madeline, frozen in place halfway to the bathroom wearing nothing but a sheet.

"Oh," his mother said, obviously surprised but not so surprised she couldn't be congenial. "Hello, there."

Chapter Nine

Madeline was beyond embarrassed. She was mortified.

Riley stood near the bed. With his hair slightly shaggy, his face unshaven, his jeans slung low and barely zipped, he could have been a walking advertisement for anything. The dog plopped his hindquarters down by the door as if readying for the grand finale.

This was not a good way to meet a man's mother.

She knew her eyes were huge, and she was probably as pale as the sheet she was wearing. She clamped her mouth shut to keep from stammering and making matters worse.

On second thought, nothing could make this worse.

Riley's mother was beautiful. Her face was heart-shaped, her eyes green, and her hair was straight and shiny as silk.

"This isn't a good time, Mom." The traces of annoyance in Riley's voice drew everyone's gaze, including the dog's.

"Yes, dear, I can see that." His mother's voice sounded strained, too.

"I just wish you would have called first."

"You mean, by phone. I wonder why I didn't think of that."

Riley had the grace to cringe a little as that point hit home. His mother turned beseeching eyes to Madeline.

"I am genuinely sorry to intrude. It's just that I've been sick with worry about Riley. All mothers worry, but it's been especially difficult after coming so close to losing him. I still have night terrors about those months." She extended one perfectly manicured hand. "I'm Chloe Merrick. This buffoon's mother."

While Madeline was jostling to secure the sheet with her other hand, Riley said, "Come on, Mom, it's not as if you haven't already spoken to her. I guess this would be as good a time as any to thank you for hiring a nurse behind my back."

Beyond the windows, the wind crooned. The waves washed noisily ashore. In the bedroom, three people and one dog stood frozen in stunned silence.

Madeline finally found her voice. "I never said your mother hired me, Riley."

She could see him trying valiantly to make sense of her statement. He could build walls and take them down and move mountains or build pyramids if he had to. This was outside his area of expertise. "If Mom didn't send you, what were you doing at the jobsite? How did you know about the heart transplant?"

Of their own volition, Madeline's eyes went to his scar. His chest rose and fell with the deep breaths he was taking. She could feel his mother looking from one to the other. She knew, as Madeline knew, that something was clicking into place in his mind.

"I think I'll leave you two alone," Chloe Merrick said. She reached her hand to her son's cheek. "Will you be all right?"

He nodded once, his jaw set.

She kissed his cheek as if she wished it would make everything better, the way it had when he was small. "You call me," she said. The or else came through loud and clear. Sparing one last look at Madeline, she turned on her heel and walked out of her son's house.

Madeline felt as if she were standing in a vacuum

where there was no sound, no movement, and no air. Riley had looked at her in so many different ways since she'd met him. She'd seen curious speculation on his face, and dark intensity, and smoldering invitation. Right now his eyes held an impassive coldness that sent a shiver up her spine.

"Your sainted fiancé, dead eighteen months. My heart transplant, eighteen months ago. It seems your Aaron and I have something in common besides you."

A lone tear ran down her face as she thought about the first time she'd laid eyes on Riley, and the first time she'd spoken to him. Yes, he'd jumped to conclusions, but she'd let him. Her intentions had been pure, for all the good it did either of them.

She'd wanted to tell him.

She'd tried to tell him.

She should have told him, *privacy laws be damned,* because a lie of omission was sometimes the most hurtful lie of all.

"I'm sorry, Riley." Before another tear could fall, she pried her feet from the floor and went in search of her clothes.

Riley didn't say a word, not when Madeline made her way to the bathroom, as regal as a queen in that damn sheet, not a few minutes later when he heard the soft fall of her footsteps coming down the hall, through his living room, to the kitchen, where he stood, his back to her.

"May I explain?" she asked.

"There's no need."

"Riley, please."

He'd pulled on his shirt. It chafed wherever it touched his skin. He wanted to rip it off and throw it. "It's a little late, don't you think? Let's not turn this into some big drama. It was never going to be more than a little sex anyway."

He heard the deep breath she took.

Turning, he looked her in the eye. "Your rent's paid through Friday. Maybe I'll see you around."

He knew he'd hurt her, knew by the deep breath she took, and by the way she walked stiffly out the door, as if any sudden moves would make her crumble.

Some immeasurable amount of time later he heard her car start on the other side of the arborvitae hedge. He saw her pull out of the end of her driveway and head south.

That was that.

She hadn't waited until Friday to leave. He had no good reason to go over there, but he cut through the damn gap in the damn hedge anyway, and let himself in. The dog followed him from room to room, as silent as he.

It was just as he'd expected. Whatever dishes she'd used had been washed and put away. Her bed was made. The closet was empty.

She was gone.

Riley walked out to the lake next and stood where she'd shed so many tears for her Aaron. Staring at an iron ore freighter lumbering across the horizon, Riley shook his head. He'd been manipulated by some of the most cunning women on the planet. There was no reason to give this one the power to cut to the bone.

Okay. So he'd thought she was different. She'd been a virgin. For a few days, she'd been exactly what he'd needed.

That didn't mean he needed her now. She'd been a diversion, and it had been fun while it lasted. He didn't appreciate being duped, but the sex was good. There was no reason to let a little duplicity cancel out a great roll in the hay.

He dropped his head into his hands, heaved a great sigh, because the sex was only part of it. If he was honest with himself, it wasn't even the best part.

Enough, he told himself. It was over. She was gone. And that was that.

He turned his phone back on when he reached his own house. He saw a missed call from Kipp, listened to what was probably meant to be a soothing message from his mother then dropped the phone on the table on the way by.

He took a good long look at every room. The clutter and grandma furnishings were gone. There was an old trunk in the living room, a huge framed mirror leaning against one wall and that horrible green-and-orange couch where they'd made love. The dining room was empty. It was just as well. The only table he used was in the kitchen, anyway. He sat down at it and stared at the scorch marks in the marred surface.

How many nights had he sat here, sipping hot coffee and waiting for morning? Was it really morning he'd been waiting for?

"You're not a tumbleweed," she'd said. "You're a tree."

Riley thought about that now. A tumbleweed was an invasive plant that grew gangly and then died from drought and sun. Eventually the incessant wind snapped it off just above the ground. What was left tumbled and rolled, sowing its weed seeds, dead, across the plains. Trees, on the other hand, put down roots. They bent in the wind, shed their leaves every fall and sprouted new ones every spring. Somehow they survived ice storms and droughts, changed by the elements, but alive.

Riley felt. Something.

He held perfectly still. In his chest there was a

tingle. A prickle as if Novocain was wearing off. His heart reared up. It gave a strange little shudder then stuttered before settling down again, heavy.

He placed his hands flat on the table's cool surface. In his chest, his heart went thump, thump, thump.

He could feel it beating.

He was alive. Because of this heart, Aaron's heart, he was alive.

The dog looked up at him as if waiting for him to say something profound. Riley couldn't have gotten a word past the knot in his throat if he'd tried.

He might have remained silent the rest of the day had the phone not rung. He grabbed it up, and the first thing to tumble out of his mouth was "Damn." Not because it rang.

Because it wasn't her.

He put it to his ear and sat up straighter. "Say that again?"

The man on the other end of the line said, "This is Hank Chester. I happened to drive through Gale this mornin'. Hadn't been up that way in a while. And I saw a sign on the light pole. That brown dog still hanging around there?"

Riley eyed the dog. "He might be."

"Is he on the ugly side, with a tail somebody did a poor job of lopping off?"

"His tail has been lopped."

"Went missing almost two months ago. It sounds like you have my dog."

After the call ended, Riley looked the dog in the eye and said, "You're going home."

The dog laid his snout on his paws. And sighed.

It was almost dark by the time Hank Chester finally pulled into Riley's driveway on Shoreline Drive. Riley was reserving judgment. Just because the man was an hour late and drove a rusted green pickup truck with a gun rack in the back window and a filthy dog crate in the bed was no reason to distrust him. He was a large man with size twelve boots and a toothpick between his brown teeth. Poor oral hygiene was no reason to distrust him, either.

Riley disliked him on sight.

He clomped all the way to the front door—he wanted to tell him to tie his damn boots—nodded at Riley, evidently his version of a greeting, then eyed the dog. "That's him, all right. Damnedest dog I ever laid eyes on."

"You're sure he's yours?" Riley asked.

"You think there are two dogs this ugly in the world?"

Riley's hands tightened into fists at his sides. He counted to ten. And reminded himself there was no law against calling a dog ugly.

"If you're sure he's yours, take him. I rounded up the things I bought for him. Here's his leash and collar, and the pillow he slept on in the kitchen. You might as well take the food, too."

The man cackled. "He slept on a pillow? What were you trying to do, turn him into a sissy dog?"

Okay. Riley wasn't in the mood to be nice anyway. He dropped the pillow and leash on the porch and closed the door at his back.

Chester took the hint. He backed up and wiped the dumb-ass grin off his face. "Get over here, mutt," he said.

The dog hung his head and skulked to Chester's side. Riley liked it better when he couldn't feel his heart.

"What's his name?" Riley asked in spite of himself.

"He doesn't answer to anything. I call him Dipstick, Stupid, Gutless Wonder."

Dislike might have been a little mild for what Riley felt for Hank Chester. But if it was his dog, it was his dog.

"Where do you live?" Riley asked. They were by the truck now, and Riley could see a logo on the door.

"Twenty-five miles south of here. This stupid dog has run away more times than I can count. Thought he was gone for good this time."

Riley couldn't look at the dog. "Twenty-five miles is a long way for a dog to run. What is it you do?"

"I'm a house painter. What's it to you?"

Riley recalled something Madeline had said about men in white coveralls. "Do you wear a white coverall?"

"Yeah, so?"

"Wait!"

The dog stopped, just stopped, and no amount of shoving on his master's part could move him.

"Not the brightest bulb, that's for damn sure." Chester brought his foot back.

"How much?" Riley said.

Hank Chester wouldn't know Riley's handmade Italian shoes from galoshes, but that Porsche in the driveway said "Chump" to him. He eyed it, and then he gave Riley a big ugly grin. "What's he worth to ya?"

If Riley had learned one thing today, it was that if there was a fool here, it wasn't Hank Chester.

"I drove all the way up here. Put miles on my truck. Gas ain't cheap, you know. Then there was all the emotional whadyacallit. Mental anguish, that's it. Hard to put a price on that."

The dog growled. Chester brought his foot back again.

Riley had the man by the throat before Chester could say, "Shut up, mutt."

"Look," Riley said, releasing him. "I haven't had a good day. So what do you say you name your price so you can get the hell out of here?"

Hank Chester didn't take too kindly to being threatened, but evidently he was smarter than he looked. He made the deal and drove away in his rusty four-by-four pickup truck, a wad of money in his beefy fist.

When it was just the two of them again, Riley finally knew what his dog had known all along. Madeline was right. It was time this loyal friend had a name.

Chapter Ten

In some far corner of Madeline's mind she was aware of birdsong and the indescribably sweet scent of apple blossoms wafting through the windows, but Orchard Hill fully enveloped in the embrace of a May morning wasn't her main concern. She had something far more pressing on her mind.

She raced through her newly rented house, careful of the boxes waiting to be unpacked. Unpacking wasn't her greatest concern this morning, either. Right now, her first priority was opening the small package she'd purchased after Summer and the boys had left last night after helping her move across town.

Hopping from foot to foot in her new bathroom, she tore the cellophane wrapper with her teeth and ripped the top of the box off then hurriedly read the directions. In almost no time, she was staring at the wand in her hand.

Negative.

She looked closer, as if to catch the results in the act of changing. The dash sign in the little window remained an unwavering blue.

She wasn't pregnant.

She read the directions again just to be sure she'd followed them correctly, for she'd been late before, but never an entire week. That negative sign left little room for doubt.

Dropping the home pregnancy kit, wand and all into the wastebasket, she let the fact that she wasn't pregnant soak in. She stared at her reflection in the mirror and tried to decide how she felt about the results.

It wasn't disappointment *or* relief she was experiencing. What then? It was hard to place a name on what she felt, because nothing had felt quite right since she'd returned home to Orchard Hill three weeks ago.

She'd left Gale quietly that day, her heart aching and her pride in a shambles. Carrying the silence with her, she'd clutched the steering wheel with both hands and relived every conversation, every kiss, every moment of those four days she'd had with Riley.

Because she'd left the radio off, she'd had no idea a tornado warning had been issued for four counties in lower Michigan. She'd practically driven into town on the tornado's tail, and had arrived to downed power lines and missing roofs and mangled trees. The O'Malleys' orchard east of town had been hit hard, but luckily for Madeline's family the tornado skirted their eastern boundary then followed the river before fizzling.

The storm had been the talk of the town ever since. By the time anybody noticed, really noticed, that Madeline was back, she'd been home long enough to make asking about her trip seem anti-climactic.

Anti-climactic was probably a good way to describe how she felt this morning. It stood to reason the pregnancy test would be negative, for Riley had seen to protection, well, all but that last time in the shower.

Tears came to her eyes. She never used to cry so easily, one of the reasons she'd been convinced the results would be a plus sign, not a negative one. Of course, she knew better than anyone that there were other reasons for her emotions to be frayed.

She missed him.

How could she miss someone she'd only known a matter of days? Okay, she'd shared more with Riley in a matter of days than she had with anyone else in her life, but it wasn't as if they had a history together.

Four days did not a history make.

He'd been shocked, understandably so, when he'd discovered her connection to Aaron and his new heart. She wasn't surprised he'd jumped to conclusions, and she wasn't surprised he'd been angry. Although she hadn't known him long, she knew him well enough to know that he didn't say things he didn't mean, not even in anger. His words had reduced their time together to meaningless sex.

It hadn't been meaningless to her.

That hurt. She was getting real tired of feeling hurt.

From now on she was taking charge of her life. Moving from the safety of the quiet attic apartment in Summer's inn had been an important step. She'd accepted a job with Emily Richmond, the new midwife in town. And she was going out with her friends more. One of these days, she might even ride the mechanical bull everyone was talking about.

She wasn't sure about bungee jumping, but scuba diving sounded like fun. She and her friends were saving for a vacation in Hawaii. She might try surfing, too.

She wasn't going to play it safe all the time anymore.

It was difficult for anybody to imagine themselves old, but she'd had a vague sense that she would own a large sleepy cat and would take up quiet activities like quilting and knitting and puzzles. Now, she was thinking she'd like a dog. She was going to live a noisy, messy life. If she made mistakes, at least she would have interesting stories to tell in her old age.

All she had to do now was stop thinking about Riley morning, noon and night. Yesterday she thought she saw his dog chasing a squirrel in a little park on Village Street. Twice she thought she'd glimpsed a silver Porsche disappearing around a corner.

Chalking it up to her imagination running wild, she looked at the boxes waiting to be unpacked. She had plenty to do today to settle into her little bungalow. She was going to enjoy living here. From now on, if she wanted to play her music loud, she could. If she wanted to walk around naked, she would.

Like someone she used to know.

That was what Riley was now, someone she used to know. In time he would be part fond memory, part figment of her imagination.

Perhaps in a hundred years.

If Madeline hurried, she would have time to return the casserole dish to her new neighbor before Summer arrived to pick her up for a girls' night at the movies. It wasn't exactly girls gone wild, but she was looking forward to the Friday evening with her friends.

She locked the door behind her and turned around, only to stop. Instantly. In her tracks.

It wasn't her imagination.

A brown dog stood in her driveway, his knobby tail wagging excitedly. Riley stood next to him, feet apart, hands on his hips, his eyes hidden behind dark glasses.

While she was recovering her equilibrium, the friendly dog pattered over to say hello. She bent down, and for the first time in three weeks she laughed aloud at the wet tongue tickling her cheek and neck.

"Heel, Gulliver," Riley said.

Wiping dog kisses off her face, tears stung Madeline's eyes. He'd named his dog, she thought. He'd called him Gulliver, like the traveler. It suited him.

Refusing to let Riley see what his unannounced visit was doing to her, she straightened her spine. What a relief, she still had a spine. Fighting the urge to fidget, she said, "What are you doing here?"

"You cut your hair."

She supposed she couldn't blame her hand for going unbidden to her hair. What else was her hand supposed to do when her brain refused to function properly?

His hair had been cut recently, too. It didn't make

him look any more civilized. Although he probably paid more for the clothes and sunglasses he was wearing than she had for her first month's rent, he'd projected the same air of in-your-face confidence in jogging pants and a faded T-shirt. Apparently he wasn't shaving every day anymore. It made him seem more rugged, more dangerous.

"How did you know where to find me? I've only lived in this house for twenty-four hours."

"I saw you moving in yesterday."

So his car hadn't been a figment of her imagination, either. "You've been following me?"

"It isn't as if I parked down the street and spied on you through binoculars."

She felt the needle poke of a guilty conscience as she marched down her driveway, her nose in the air. She almost made it past him before his hand snagged her arm.

Her heart lurched; her body remembered his touch. She couldn't see his eyes through his dark glasses, but she could see a vein pulsing in his neck, could sense the change in his breathing, too.

"What are you doing here, Riley?" she asked again.

"You left before those five days were up."

She bristled and shook his arm off. "The time has expired."

She could have kissed Summer when she pulled up

just then. Head held high, Madeline walked the remaining distance to the curb and got in the waiting car.

She couldn't help glancing out the window as
they drove away. Riley had removed his dark glasses
and was looking at her, the leash in his right hand,
an expression of dark intensity on his lean face.

"Who was that?" Summer Matthews had a deep
sultry voice that could make ordering a sandwich
sound like a dark secret.

"Gulliver." Madeline sniffled at the poignancy of
it all.

Madeline and Summer were the same size, from
their rings, to their clothes, even their shoes. They
understood one another better than any sister could
have, but even Summer was having trouble following Madeline's train of thought. "Is Gulliver his first
name or last?"

"Gulliver is the dog," Madeline explained. "The
man is Riley Merrick."

Summer's eyebrows rose in two perfect arches
above her large hazel eyes. "What's he doing here?"

When she'd first arrived home three weeks ago,
Madeline had described Riley's house, his car, his
dog, his friend, even his mother to Summer in great
detail, but all she'd said about sex was that she'd had
it. Sometimes what a person didn't say said the most.

"I'm not sure," Madeline said thoughtfully. His

mention of their five days had alluded to sex, but he'd probably done that to gage her reaction. What *was* he doing in Orchard Hill?

"Aren't you curious?" Summer asked.

"Are you kidding? It was all I could do to get in this car and let you drive away."

The former Madeline, the one living the safe, orderly life would have stayed in the driveway making understanding noises with her tongue. She would have made this easy for Riley. But the Madeline just beginning to emerge, the one destined to live a noisy, messy and full life was going to wait to see what he was going to do next.

She put the empty casserole dish on her lap so she could rub her hands together. Her new messy life was already getting interesting.

Word traveled fast. The man who'd received Aaron Andrews's heart was in Orchard Hill.

It was Riley Merrick this and Riley Merrick that.

At first everyone spoke his name in a whisper, as if to soften the imminent pain the mention of him and how he pertained to Aaron's heart would undoubtedly incur. They didn't know that Madeline had known his identity since the night Aaron died.

It started with the clerk at the window in the post office where she went to change her mailing address on Saturday morning. "Now Madeline," Celia Bundy said, her double chin quivering above the collar of her postal uniform, "I don't know how to tell you this, so I'll just come out and say it. There's a man in town. Asking questions."

"What kind of questions?" Madeline asked.

"About Aaron." This was delivered with a gentle pat on Madeline's shoulder. "It's the man who got his heart, dear. His name is Riley Merrick."

"What did you tell him?"

Luckily nobody was behind her in line, because Celia, whose husband, Raymond, had been the chief of police until his retirement last year, launched into the tale she'd shared with Riley about the time somebody had painted the f-word and signed Madeline's name on the rusted old water tower the city had deserted years earlier. Aaron had gotten caught with white paint on his hands. Nobody could believe it, but evidence was evidence.

"To this day Raymond remembers how you rode your bicycle to the police station and dragged him outside and asked him to take you to the old water tower. Of course, we all felt bad for you, having lost your mom and dad like you did. Not even that tough old bird could deny your tearful request. Imagine Ray's surprise when he got there and saw that the profanity had been painted over with white paint."

With a sniffle, Celia said, "You and Aaron always did watch out for each other."

Madeline felt a shiver go up her spine, but she smiled gently and said, "Yes, we did."

Bonnie, the checker at the IGA store, patted Madeline's shoulder, too, only she'd shared a different story about Aaron, this one about the winning curve ball he'd pitched in the final game their senior year. By the time Madeline walked into The Hill, the restaurant where she was meeting Summer and two other friends for lunch, she'd heard Riley Merrick's name a dozen times.

The Hill was nothing like Fiona's Bistro in Gale. If a person wanted finer dining in Orchard Hill, they drove across the river to the college side of town. The Hill's décor was Americana Diner. The tables were square, the food was fresh and hot, and the service was good. As usual, the place was packed today.

Summer, Chelsea Reynolds and Abby Fitzpatrick were already seated when Madeline arrived. Chelsea and Abby looked worriedly at her as she slid onto the bench seat next to Summer. "Have you heard?" Chelsea asked.

Before Madeline could answer, the object of discussion appeared at their table. "Hello, Madeline," Riley said.

She looked up at him, for surely he'd been following her again. "There are laws against stalking," she said.

"I just finished my lunch." He pointed to a table across the aisle set with a used place setting for one.

Chelsea and Abby looked from the well-dressed Adonis to Madeline. They had no idea who he was. And yet they slid over to make room for him.

Before taking the seat opposite Madeline, he slanted them both one of his devastating smiles, the one that showcased the shape of his wide mouth and called attention to the slight indentation in his chin. "It seems the cat's got Madeline's tongue. I'm Riley Merrick. I'm the guy who got Aaron's heart."

Madeline could appreciate the way Abby's and Chelsea's mouths were hanging open. "You're making quite an impact on the town," she said.

"It's nice to know you're still a fan."

"Do you two know each other?" Abby asked.

He looked to Madeline to answer.

"It's a long story," she said.

Riley hadn't intended to interrupt Madeline's lunch with her friends, but he'd seen her saunter in. She wore black slacks that fit her like a pair of kid gloves, black sandals and a deep red shirt that hugged her torso and made her hair, which now just touched her shoulders, look like spun gold. His Neanderthal instincts had kicked in. He wanted everyone in Orchard Hill to know who he was. More importantly, he wanted everyone to know who he was to Madeline. He wanted to stake his claim right there in the restaurant. But he didn't.

Not yet.

Yesterday he'd driven from one end of Orchard Hill to the other, getting a feel for the lay of the land. It wasn't as small as he'd expected. According to the city map he'd picked up at the historical society, Orchard Hill had more than one hundred houses on the historic registry and more than twenty-thousand residents. College students accounted for almost half of that number, and lived near campus across the river. This side of town belonged to people with deep roots and long memories.

This was Madeline's side.

He could hardly believe it had been three weeks since he'd seen her. His memories didn't do her justice. He had a lot to make up for, and a lot to prove.

He started with the truth. "I'm a changed man." He could feel the other three looking at him, but he kept his gaze trained on Madeline. "I've done everything you suggested. I named my dog. I'm living in my house. And I can feel my heart beating."

"You can?" she asked.

He got the distinct impression she'd meant to say,

"That's nice." She wasn't going to make this easy for him. He was glad about that, for nothing warmed him like a good challenge, nothing except her, that is.

One of her friends, he was pretty sure her name was Abby, said, "Does it take time to regain feeling after a transplant?"

"Not normally," he answered. "In fact, I've never heard of another case like mine."

"So this sensation of being able to feel your organ is fairly recent. Ow." The petite blonde with a pixie haircut and evidently a little pixie dust in her head rubbed her shin and glared at Summer, who was sitting across from her. "Kindly take your mind out of the gutter."

Summer Matthews was the only person Riley had encountered who'd refused to talk to him. When he told her his name at the Orchard Inn, she'd closed the registration book and said there were no vacancies. He smelled a lie, and where there was a lie, there was a reason. Summer wasn't from Orchard Hill. She and Madeline looked nothing alike, and yet they were protective of one another. They reminded Riley of him and Kipp.

Madeline could see Riley taking stock of her friends. She didn't know what she would do without them, any of them. She understood Abby's curiosity, because she couldn't contain hers, either. Riley could feel his heart. Madeline wanted to know when, how, why. "How recent?" she asked him, drawing his attention.

"Since shortly after my mother walked in on us. By the way, Mom says hello."

Madeline felt herself getting warm. It wasn't embarrassment. It was surprise and the first stirring of desire.

He was good at this. She'd known it the first day she'd met him.

Riley stood and smiled around the table. "It was nice meeting all of you." He looked at Madeline last. "I'll be in touch."

Four pairs of eyes watched him saunter away. And then three pairs turned to stare at Madeline.

"His mother walked in on you? You mean, during sex?" Chelsea asked.

"You and Riley had sex? Oh my God," Abby exclaimed. "Did Aaron know?"

Since Madeline was blonde, too, she couldn't blame Abby's airheadedness on that. "Of course not. It was last month," she said. "Remember when I went to the lakeshore? Well, I drove up to Gale. I had no intention of meeting Riley. I thought that once I saw the man in possession of Aaron's beating heart I could start to believe in goodness again."

"But you met him, Riley Merrick, I mean," Chelsea said.

"How else could she have slept with him?" Abby pointed her finger in warning at Summer.

"Out with it," Chelsea said to Madeline.

"Yes," Abby agreed. "We want the story. Don't even think about leaving out a single detail."

In a quiet voice, Madeline retold the entire tale. Even Summer, who'd already heard it, leaned forward to better hear.

Madeline recalled driving out of Orchard Hill by the light of the waning moon, and how easily she'd discovered the hidden lane she'd been looking for near Gale, and how she'd felt the quiet chiming of something sweet and delicate sprinkling into the empty spaces inside her when she'd first come face-to-face with Riley. She told them about his dog and his house and his smiles. And she told them how he never pressured her, how he'd left the decision up to her, and how she knew that if she didn't make love with him that night she would regret it for the rest of her life. She included Riley's mother's unexpected visit, and concluded with Riley's reaction once the truth was out in the open.

She sighed when she was finished. Her friends sighed, too.

"You're in love with him, aren't you?" Chelsea asked.

Summer met Madeline's gaze.

Abby nodded emphatically. "When you were at the lakeshore, you were worried he would think you only loved him because of Aaron's heart. What's he doing here?"

"I don't know," Madeline said.

She planned to find out. And she planned to do it soon.

Chapter Eleven

Madeline wasn't watching where she was going when she left the restaurant. Luckily, she somehow managed to avoid running into other diners and the frazzled waitress named Roxy, who'd worked the lunch crowd as long as Madeline could remember.

As dazed as she was, she noticed Riley leaning against the building the second she stepped outside, though, the sun-warmed bricks at his back, Gulliver at his feet. His gaze never wavered from her as she neared.

She saw Riley push away from the corner, a marvelous shifting of lean muscles and smoldering man.

He started toward her, his sunglasses in his hand, Gulliver at his side. They took their half out of the middle of the sidewalk, purpose in Riley's every step, and stopped directly in front of her.

She saw everything, but honestly, she never saw the kiss coming. But kiss her he did, right there on Village Street in front of God and everyone.

Her bag slipped off her shoulder and slid down her arm, landing on the sidewalk with a quiet plop. She left it there, and went up on tiptoe, diving into a frenzied kiss. Oh, she'd missed this.

Her hands glided around his waist, her body straining against his. She felt his arms slip her around back, too, but she was most aware of his lips on hers. It was a hard kiss, a deep kiss, an I'll-die-if-I-don't-do-this-kiss that lit up the pair of them on the sidewalk better than any neon sign.

They weren't exactly living in the dark ages, and it wasn't as if everybody watching hadn't seen far more explicit embraces on the soaps or at the movies. But they didn't normally see this sort of kissing on the streets of Orchard Hill in the middle of the day.

Four heads appeared at the barbershop window, two others in curlers at the hair salon next door. Brett Avery at the hardware store stopped pricing out lawnmowers and looked, too. Edith Wilson, the sternest librarian to ever shake her finger at an errant third grader stopped on the library steps and stared, and so did anybody else who still had at least one decent eye. And every person who witnessed that red-hot kiss was going to tell somebody. It was the way of small towns. For better or for worse, news traveled fast.

Their darling Madeline was in a liplock with that charming Riley Merrick. Nobody could say for sure who'd started it, but it was obvious to everybody that this was no first kiss.

Madeline wasn't smiling when it ended. She was reeling.

"What did you do that for?" she asked. The insinuation that it had been Riley's doing might have held more weight if she hadn't had to consciously remove her arms from around his neck in order to put a little distance between them.

"I couldn't help myself," he said.

She still didn't know why he was in town or how long he planned to stick around, but lordy, she hadn't been able to help herself, either. "Where are you staying?"

She could see him visibly trying to pull himself together after that kiss, too. "Not in your friend's inn," he said.

She supposed that made as much sense as could be

expected. She came within a hairbreadth of asking him if he wanted to come back to her house with her.

As if reading her mind, he said, "I have a little more unfinished business to take care of. Through it all I'm getting to know all the people who know and love you in Orchard Hill. There are a lot of them."

"Riley, we need to talk."

"Yes, we do. Will you be home later?" He took a step back, away from her, and called Gulliver.

"Where are you going?" she asked.

The wind lifted his hair off his forehead and fluttered his collar at his throat. "There's one more person I have to see."

Madeline had been afraid of that.

She was going to stop trying to make sense of her life. She was also going to stop expecting the next person who knocked on her door to be Riley.

That didn't mean she could hide her complete astonishment when she opened her door to Aaron's parents. She'd known Jim and Connie Andrews since she'd accepted his invitation to attend a Halloween party at his house when she was twelve. She'd eaten supper at their table and slept in their spare room, as comfortable in front of their television growing up as she'd been in front of hers.

Jim Andrews was tall and stocky. Aaron had

gotten his height from his father, but in every other way, he'd resembled his mom. Both had been born with blue eyes, blond hair and ready smiles.

Connie hadn't smiled much these past eighteen months. "I know you're busy," she said gently. "But may we come in, dear?"

Madeline came to her senses. "Of course. Of course you can come in. By all means, come in." She couldn't help looking past them out the door. There was no wavy-haired man in sight.

Please, God, she prayed, *don't let them ask me to honor Aaron's memory a little longer.*

"We heard you were moving," Jim said, looking around for a comfortable place to sit.

Madeline moved a box off her overstuffed chair.

"And we heard you took a job with a new doctor in town, too," Connie said, taking a seat on the sofa near her husband.

Oh, God, Madeline thought. Here it came. "No matter how many things change, I'll always love Aaron," she said. And she meant every word.

"Oh, we know that, dear. You're a good girl. That isn't why we're here." Connie looked at her husband. They took a collective breath.

He nodded in moral support, and she continued. "I always worried that you would find someone else. Selfish of me, I know, but a mother can't help being selfish sometimes. And then we had a visitor today. The young man who has Aaron's heart."

Madeline sank to the sofa, too.

"He has a heart of gold, that one. He's like Aaron that way. He listened to our stories about raising Aaron. We showed him the photo albums. And watching his face, knowing a part of our boy lives on, well, we both felt a weight lift."

Madeline didn't even try to check her tears.

Connie stood. It took Jim a minute to get the hint, but he found his feet, too.

"We saw you two, er, ah, in front of the restaurant," Jim said, despite the elbow he took in his stomach. "Well, we did," he said defensively. "And we both want you to know you have our blessing."

Madeline was crying freely now. She hugged them both at the door, sniffled in both their ears. "I'll always love Aaron. And I'll always love you two, too."

"You'd better!" Jim said.

They all laughed, Madeline and Connie through their tears. Madeline saw Jim wipe his eyes, too, after he was outside.

She had their blessing, she thought, closing the door behind Aaron's parents. Talk about putting the cart before the horse.

Her next visitor wasn't Riley, either. This one didn't bother to knock. Madeline's great-aunt

Eleanor thundered in, a long garment bag fluttering behind her.

"It's all over town. Bound to happen sooner or later," she said, turning in a circle with so much vehemence Madeline felt the air turbulence.

"Aunt Eleanor, it's nice to see you. What do you have there?"

Eleanor Montgomery had been Madeline's height in her day. In her eighties now, she'd grown shorter and wider with every passing decade. She was as daunting as she'd ever been, however.

"Why, it's your mama's wedding gown, of course. I've been holding on to it, and it's a good thing I have, too."

She hung the garment bag from the parlor door.

"You're young. What's done is done."

"Aunt Eleanor, what are you talking about?"

The gray-haired woman lowered her voice to a stage whisper. "I'm talking about your virginity. Anybody with half a brain can tell you're hot for that boy who ended up with Aaron's heart. Don't get me wrong. Sex is and always has been too much fun to resist. Oh, girls in my day claimed they beat the beaus off with a big stick, but a lot of us didn't. Your great-uncle Herbert was a rascal, that one."

She twittered.

Madeline couldn't help it. She just couldn't picture Uncle Herbert and Aunt Eleanor having sex without cringing a little.

"Anyhoo," Eleanor said, facing her great-niece the way Madeline's mama or grandma would have if they hadn't died too young. "The thing you have to do now is grab your young man by the, well, by whatever you can get a hold of, and get yourselves both down to the church. It's human nature to enjoy sex. My only advice to you girls nowadays is don't give it away free."

Madeline didn't know how an eighty-year-old widow as solid as a brick wall could move like a whirlwind, but that was the impression she left as she headed for the door. "Heed my advice. And don't let your young man see that dress until you're on your way down the aisle."

With a pat on Madeline's cheek, the old woman was gone.

Well, Madeline thought, standing in the wake of that storm. She had a blessing, sage advice and an heirloom gown.

The only thing missing was Riley's profession of love.

She could tell it was Riley at the door by his knock. She opened the door, and stood back, wanting a little space for some reason.

He sauntered in with that legendary swagger and

an expression to match. Underneath, he was just a man. Madeline reminded herself of that as she waited for him to speak.

He did, eventually, but not until he'd looked around her living room. "This was built before mine was, wasn't it? It's nice."

It didn't feel like home yet to her. It felt more like Grand Central Station.

"What's that?" he asked, pointing to the garment bag still hanging over the parlor door.

"My mother's wedding gown."

"Okay," he said.

"What do you mean okay?"

Riley looked more closely at Madeline. She didn't appear to be in a good mood. It was probably too much to hope for to think he wasn't to blame for that. He was doing everything in his power to do this right, but he was winging it here. "I don't mean anything," he said. "You're angry. Why?"

"Why? *Why? Why.* I'll tell you why. You show up in town out of the blue, kiss me senseless like some damn caveman, then rush away without an explanation. Everybody knows. Evidently you're hot and I'm, well, from now on I'm not supposed to give it away free. Where have you been, anyway?"

Riley had done something to upset her. He wasn't sure what exactly, but Madeline didn't get upset for no reason.

He walked closer, reached for her hand, and held it as he said, "I went to the cemetery. Aaron and I had a little heart-to-heart."

He didn't mean to make her cry.

"What did you two talk about?" she asked.

"Actually I did most of the talking." He was hoping for a smile but settled for a roll of her eyes. "I didn't know who else to ask."

"Ask what?" she said.

"For your hand."

"You mean, as in marriage?" She squeezed his fingers tighter with every word.

It bordered on painful. She was a strong woman. He didn't see how he could love her any more. He could barely contain everything he felt for her. His heart hammered in his chest in what felt like an arterial burst of love.

"Yeah," he said. "Will you?" His voice sounded husky in his own ears, his body warming by degrees, the sound of distant drums echoing more loudly with every breath he took. She smelled wonderful. He didn't even know what perfume she wore. It was flowery, sexy.

Very gently, she drew her hand from his. Very softly, she took a deep breath. Very calmly, she raised those blue eyes of hers to his and said, "Give me one good reason why I should marry you, Riley Merrick."

It wasn't the response he was waiting for. It sure as hell wasn't the one he'd been hoping for. He ran through the request in his mind, trying to decide where he'd gone wrong. God help him, it was all wrong. Okay, he was going to start again.

"Madeline—"

Just then there was a little skirmish on her front porch. Three men he didn't recognize jostled each other to be the first through the door. Once inside, they stood three abreast, a solid wall of shoulders and brawn.

"Are you Riley Merrick?" the one in the middle said.

"Boys, this isn't a good time," Madeline said.

Boys? he thought. Obviously, she knew them. "I am," Riley said.

"You're all everyone's talking about," the one on the right practically growled.

"I don't like what people are saying," the one on the left countered.

Who the hell were they? And what business was this of theirs?

"They're saying you've slept with our baby sister," the guy in the middle declared.

Baby sister? Uh-oh.

With every statement, the Sullivan men took a step closer to Riley. With every step they took, Madeline said, "Hold it right there."

She finally threw herself between him and them. Riley found it encouraging that she didn't want to see him killed. "Don't worry, honey," he whispered close to her ear. "I can handle this."

She threw up her hands and stepped aside. "Riley, these are my brothers. Marsh. Reed. And Noah. He's all yours, boys. Just don't leave any evidence. I'm only renting this place."

The wind had shifted. Instead of the scent of apple blossoms wafting on the air, Riley smelled trouble.

The three Sullivan men looked capable of defending their baby sister's honor. Riley heard water rushing over rocks in the distance. He hadn't known her lot bordered the river, but eyeing the three men waiting to tear him to shreds, he decided it might be wise to stay away from the water.

The oldest one, Marsh, looked the most like an orchard grower, if there was such a type. He was as tall as Riley but outweighed him by a good twenty pounds. He was in his mid-thirties. His sideburns were dark beneath his ball cap, and he had the kind of tan a man acquired working outside season after season. His jeans were faded, his eyes brown, his gaze direct and assessing. His fingers squeezed into fists at his sides. Oh, yeah, he was ready to tear Riley limb from limb.

The second one, Reed, had the tall, lanky build of a race car driver. He was a masculine version of Madeline, blond hair, blue eyes. There were no visible scars or calluses on his hands. This man worked with his mind. He looked as if he was going to enjoy kicking Riley's ass.

The third brother, Noah, looked younger than Riley. He had the loose-jointed devil-may-care stance of a man who enjoyed a good barroom brawl. This one knew how to fight, and he knew how to fight dirty.

They walked closer, as if daring Riley to turn tail and run. He'd left Gulliver sleeping in his motel room. Now he wished he'd have brought him along.

He held his ground, and kept them all in his sight.

He didn't appreciate their interference, and felt his adrenaline kicking in. He reminded himself they were Madeline's brothers. They'd been with her through every upheaval in her life. They believed he'd taken advantage of their baby sister.

Seeing a curtain move at a window in Madeline's house, he decided to cut to the chase. "Who do I ask for her hand?"

The Sullivan men looked at him the way Madeline sometimes did. There was no mistaking the family resemblance.

Apparently Marsh was the spokesperson for the group. "You're willing to marry Madeline?"

"Willing, hell. I'm not sure she'll have me. I was in the middle of proposing when you three barged in."

"You slept with our sister. What do you expect?"

Obviously they weren't going to let him off the hook completely.

"She was vulnerable," Noah said.

"Innocent," Marsh declared.

Talking about it was getting them worked up more.

"I love her," Riley said.

"Then you should have waited." This came from Reed.

"Are you three married?" Riley asked.

Three men hemmed and hawed.

"I don't suppose any of you are waiting to get to the altar." He looked them in the eye one by one.

"All right," Marsh said, knowing when it was time to move on. "You say you love her and you want to marry her. Tell us this. What the hell took you so long to come here?"

Until three weeks ago, Riley wouldn't have answered. He wouldn't have considered Madeline's older brothers' feelings. It wasn't that he'd been cold or hard—fine, maybe he'd been a little cold and hard, but he wouldn't have believed he owed them an explanation. After all, what he'd shared with Madeline had been between the two of them. It had been sex, and it had been powerful. And private.

Marsh, Reed and Noah Sullivan weren't asking about sex. Hell, they probably preferred to pretend they didn't know anything about their baby sister's sex life. That was the trouble with pretending. Eventually the truth grabbed pretense by the throat and squeezed until every last thin excuse gasped and surrendered to what was real.

And what was real to Riley was more than the sex he'd had with Madeline. Yeah, he'd been duped. Madeline had lied by omission, and he'd been mad as hell. Dammit, he'd had every right to be mad. At least that was what he'd told himself that first week after she left. Just one more thin excuse that bit the dust once she was gone.

Gone.

That was how it had felt. She'd gone. Just gone. Like a stream of vapor thinning in a ray of sunlight or a dream that became hazy upon awakening. She'd gone. And every place she'd been was a memory. Her laughter in his kitchen. Her tears by the lake. Her image on his sofa, at his table, in his shower and in his bed.

But those weren't the most indelible marks she'd made on him, for she'd left her imprint on every facet of his life. Because of her, he could feel his heart beating. She'd gotten to him, touched him in a way he'd never been touched.

She loved him.

He'd thought about this. A lot. He'd been an arrogant jackass when he'd told her they had five days together. "Five days," he'd said, cocky as hell. "If you leave now, you'll never know what might have happened during those five days."

Looking back now, he was surprised she hadn't left then and there. But she hadn't. And he was pretty sure it was because she loved him.

Please, God, let that be the reason.

He didn't know what he'd ever done to deserve a woman like her. Right now, her three older brothers deserved the truth.

Riley looked the eldest Sullivan in the eye first, and then the other two. "The first week after she left I walked around, growling like a grizzly just coming out of hibernation. I tried telling myself my house, my chest, my life wasn't empty without her. These past two weeks, I've been calculating and planning. I figure a woman like Madeline is only going to give me one shot, if I'm lucky."

They looked at Riley long and hard. Next they looked at each other. "Let's get you back inside so you can make an honest woman out of Madeline," Marsh said.

The other two nodded.

They had it all wrong. Riley was hoping she would make an honest man out of him.

The Sullivans followed Riley inside. Madeline got up out of an overstuffed chair as if she'd been there all along.

"We've reached a little understanding with Junior, here," the only one of the bunch younger than Riley stated.

"It'll all work out," Marsh assured her.

"Just hear him out," Reed insisted.

"Give him a chance."

"You can thank us later."

Riley lost track of who said what.

They each took a turn hugging their sister. Each of them shot Riley a meaningful look over her head.

Not one of them fooled Madeline.

"Where were we?" Riley said after they left.

She looked at him, her eyes wide and blue and intelligent. Hands on her hips, she said, "I asked you to give me one good reason why I should marry you, Riley Merrick."

Chapter Twelve

Madeline was the bravest woman Riley had ever known, but this haughtiness was a front. This bold, daring young woman was afraid of Riley's answer. He'd hurt her when he'd reduced everything they'd had to sex.

She'd made him see himself so clearly. She'd brought a sense of order to his house and had brought out of hiding a sense of commitment to his dog.

She was smart.

She was brave.

She was the best thing that had ever happened to him.

She wanted one good reason? Why should she marry him?

Riley knew that once he got started, he could list a hundred reasons he loved her.

He went to the window. He didn't know why, but the outdoors seemed to be beckoning. He'd been outdoors when he'd met her. He'd been outdoors when he'd first kissed her. It seemed to him that something this momentous needed to be said outdoors, too.

Checking the front pocket of his jeans, he said, "Would you come outside with me, Madeline?"

She didn't acquiesce immediately. When she did, she did so without saying a word.

She moved blithely ahead of him—a tree, too, but a willow, able to sway and bend without breaking. She led the way through her house, down four steps, stopping on an old flagstone patio. There she faced him bravely.

She'd lived and loved and lost. He'd known it, but he hadn't felt the depth of her loss until he'd stood at Aaron's grave today.

It had humbled him, moved him, changed him.

Until today, Riley would have rejected the notion that the shaft of sunlight that suddenly found its way through a narrow passageway in the clouds wasn't a random occurrence. Now he knew that none of this was random.

He took her hand, relieved that she let him. Of course, just then a lawn mower was started next door.

"Is there some place we can go where we won't be interrupted?" he asked.

She looked at him. And then she looked around. She pointed to a slight gap in the underbrush beyond her lawn. "That path leads to the river."

Of course, he thought, saying nothing as they followed the path. When they emerged, they were standing in a little glen secluded on three sides, open to the river and the sky.

Suddenly nerves shot to his throat. He had to clear it in order to begin. "You asked why you should marry me?"

Her eyes were as pale as the sky, her lashes dark against her skin. She started tapping her foot impatiently. It was all he could do to keep from swinging her off her feet.

"Everybody in this town believes you're an angel. Nobody knows you like I do."

Her foot stilled and her chin came up slightly. He had her attention.

"It's no coincidence that Aaron gave me his heart and then filled it with you."

"Then this is about Aaron?" she asked.

"Hell no."

Her eyebrows rose a fraction.

"His heart lives on in me and his memory lives on in you and everyone else in this town, but even if I reject his heart tomorrow and by some new miracle receive another, I would still love you, I would still want you, I would still want to write your name across the sky."

Now her throat quivered and her eyes watered.

"You're a beautiful vibrant angel of a woman with a streak of bad-girl coursing through your veins. Yes, I was your first lover, but that isn't the reason I want you to marry me, either. Marry me, Madeline, because you're the first, the only woman I've ever loved. Marry me, and I promise I will spend the rest of my life doing everything in my power to make you glad you did."

Tears ran down her face now. On a sniffle, she said, "Darn you, Riley Merrick."

"Is that a yes?" he asked, wiping her cheek with his thumb.

"How can I say no to that?"

They'd kissed so many times, but they didn't kiss now. Riley did the only thing he could do. His arms went around her waist and he swung her around, spinning them both, the breeze gentle, the sun warm, the river too intent upon its journey to pay the lovers on its bank any attention.

Madeline relished the feel of the strong arms

around her, the sound of water rushing around the bend and the sight of the world spinning. Whoa. "Riley, you'd better put me down. This twirling is making me queasy."

He put her down, but he didn't release her. They stayed that way, her eyes closed, her cheek on his chest, her ear pressed to his beating heart. "Even if you rejected Aaron's heart tomorrow and received another," she said quietly. "I would love you the same. No matter whose heart beats in your chest, my heart is yours."

She felt the change in him. His arms tightened around her and his breathing deepened. Her dizziness had passed, and desire was unfurling in her toes, among other fun places.

She breathed in his scent, reveling in the possessiveness in the touch of his hands on her back, his breath warm against her ear. There was something she had to tell him, and she had to do it soon, because any second now this living breathing passion they shared was going to wipe out every thought except one. "I'm pretty sure I'm pregnant."

It took a full five seconds for her words to register. She could feel his reluctance even then.

Raising her eyes innocently to his dark, hooded ones, she said, "The home pregnancy kit said I wasn't. But a woman knows."

She watched it sink in. As one second followed another, his expression changed in the subtlest of ways. First there was confusion, then a query, then a light, and finally a grin.

"That time in the shower," he said. "Do you know that was my favorite time?"

Any second now he was going to start strutting.

He lifted his face to the sky and let loose a re-sounding, "Yes!"

An instant later his expression changed. "Are you all right? Do you need to lie down?"

"No," she said. A light came into her eyes, too. "Well, maybe lying down is a good idea."

Riley knew what was on Madeline's mind by the tone of her voice and the hint of a dimple in her right cheek. He didn't know what he'd ever done to deserve her, to deserve any of this, to be the recipient of Aaron's heart and of her love or her passion.

Who was he to deny her?

They walked together past the briars and under-brush, then went inside hand-in-hand. She showed him the way up the stairs to her bedroom. After that, they took turns leading, giving and receiving.

Somehow their clothes came off. They smiled and moved and kissed, eager and warm, willing and hungry after their three weeks apart. Their arms and legs tangled, drawing toward one another, her heart beating against his. They melded together like they always did, passion raining down and fireworks shooting through the sky.

Sometime later, when they were both breathing evenly and Madeline was thinking marvelous thoughts, Riley got out of bed and reached for his jeans. Curious, she sat up, the sheet falling to her waist.

After retrieving something, he kicked the jeans aside then climbed in next to her again. He opened his hand, and in it was a ruby necklace, the biggest, brightest ruby Madeline had ever seen.

Her mouth was open, and her latest peculiarity, tears, ran down her cheeks. "Oh, Riley."

"I didn't buy a diamond ring yet, in case you wanted to help choose it. But even if you would have said no to my marriage proposal, I would have given you this."

He held the necklace up, letting the lamplight catch it. He put it on her, his fingers slightly clumsy as he tried to work the intricate clasp. She waited patiently while his fingertips tickled the back of her neck, the cool ruby warming against her skin.

When Riley was finished, he faced her. She looked back at him, blue eyes beaming, her neck long and graceful, the pale skin on her chest taking on a red hue from the glowing ruby. Her breasts were creamy white and fuller than they'd been three weeks ago, her ribs showing slightly below them, her waist narrow above the flair of her hips that disappeared beneath the sheet.

"What are you doing?" she asked.

He couldn't believe she could still be bashful after making love as they had. "I'm putting you to memory," he said. "How soon will you marry me?"

She smiled, a devilish light coming into her eyes. "Hmm," she said in a sultry voice, "It so happens I already have a dress."

She leaned forward and kissed him. He eased backward, bringing her with him, the mattress shifting at his back, Madeline working her magic everywhere she touched, and Riley working his magic, too.

"Does that mean you'll marry me soon?"

"I would love that, Riley. Yes, soon."

They had much to discuss, such as where they would live and work, for she'd just taken a new job. But those were small obstacles and could wait.

The rest of the wedding plans would have to wait, too.

Right now this was what mattered most. This woman. And this man. Together, and deeply in love.

Outside their window the earth sighed. The clouds parted and a joyous May moon floated into view.

Epilogue

Anybody walking past the stone church on Briar Street in Orchard Hill on Friday evening would have seen candlelight flickering in the stained-glass windows. Not that anybody was walking by. It seemed everybody was inside waiting for the wedding to begin.

The pure melodious notes of the flutist swirled like the stir of anticipation. Vases filled with blossom-tipped branches from the Sullivans' orchard adorned the altar. More sprigs of apple blossoms were tucked into the bows on the end of every pew.

Riley's mother beamed as the usher brought her

to her seat. Both his stepmothers nodded at her as she slid in next to them.

Four men in dark suits stepped out of the vestibule and took their places at the front of church. The moment everyone was waiting for was almost upon them.

Kipp patted his pocket, checking to make sure the rings were still there. Riley's brothers looked nervous, too.

Not Riley. Staring out at the faces of his large, extended family, and at Madeline's three older brothers sitting in the front row, and her friends and aunts and uncles and cousins, he knew no fear. Madeline had taught him that.

In the absence of fear, he stood waiting for the best thing that had ever happened to him to appear. The flute music changed to the heavenly strains from a single violin, and the procession of bridesmaids began.

First came Abby Fitzpatrick, a petite blonde with stars in her eyes and her sights set on Riley's younger brother. Next was Chelsea Reynolds, a curvy brunette who was wishing she hadn't sworn off men. Madeline's maid of honor came last. Summer Matthews floated up the aisle like royalty. Ignoring the smirk on Riley's older brother's face, she took her place beside her friends and looked back at the double doors at the back of the church.

The moment everyone was waiting for dawned.

The double doors opened. And there stood Madeline on Aaron's father's arm. It was difficult for Riley to believe he hadn't always been able to feel his heart, for it beat so steady and strong and true.

Madeline was the picture of her mother—later everyone would say so—in her mom's silk gown. To Riley, she was a vision, his vision of the future.

She fairly floated up the aisle, the bravest woman he'd even known. Her gaze was on his, and his alone, her hair fluttering in the same invisible breeze that was causing the candlelight to flicker. The satin of her dress had darkened slightly to the color of the evening air. The gown had no train and she wore no veil. Her only adornment was the ruby necklace nestled between her collarbones, and the love in her eyes.

Madeline couldn't take her eyes off Riley. His face was clean-shaven, his eyes dark and honest, his shirt white against his tanned skin, his suit black and his shoulders broad. The past two weeks had been a whirlwind, with everyone asking questions and making suggestions for their big day. She and Riley couldn't have pulled off a big church wedding in only two weeks without them. Through it all, they'd remained calm and serene.

She was aware of much sniffling throughout the church behind her as Aaron's dad kissed her cheek and placed her hand in Riley's. Today Madeline's eyes remained dry. She knew, as she'd known a handful of times in her life, that she was exactly where she was meant to be at this precise moment in time. The universe told her with every flicker of candlelight. Even if she hadn't been able to see it, she would have felt it in the love drawing her to Riley's side.

Later she wouldn't remember the reverend's exact words, but she would never forget the sound of Riley's voice, and hers, as they promised to love, honor and cherish each other as long as they both lived.

It was a simple ceremony that acknowledged something extraordinary. For despite the chaos and lightning speed of this modern world, two people out of billions had found each other and fallen in love.

Madeline smiled at Riley as the reverend said, "You may kiss the bride."

They'd talked about this, had rehearsed this, because it was no secret to anybody that their kisses tended to spin out of control. Standing before all the people she knew and loved, and who knew and loved her in return, she lifted her face as her new husband lowered his.

Madeline's and Riley's eyes closed as their lips touched, so they didn't see the ruby necklace glow brighter, but many of their guests saw. And everybody in that old stone church on Briar Street heard the chiming of something sweet and delicate sprinkling down around each and every one of them.

* * * * *

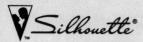

COMING NEXT MONTH

Available June 29, 2010

#2053 McFARLANE'S PERFECT BRIDE
Christine Rimmer
Montana Mavericks: Thunder Canyon Cowboys

#2054 WELCOME HOME, COWBOY
Karen Templeton
Wed in the West

#2055 ACCIDENTAL FATHER
Nancy Robards Thompson

#2056 THE BABY SURPRISE
Brenda Harlen
Brides & Babies

#2057 THE DOCTOR'S UNDOING
Gina Wilkins
Doctors in Training

#2058 THE BOSS'S PROPOSAL
Kristin Hardy
The McBains of Grace Harbor

REQUEST YOUR FREE BOOKS!
2 FREE NOVELS PLUS 2 FREE GIFTS!

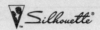

SPECIAL EDITION
Life, Love and Family!

YES! Please send me 2 FREE Silhouette® Special Edition® novels and my 2 FREE gifts (gifts are worth about $10). After receiving them, if I don't wish to receive any more books, I can return the shipping statement marked "cancel." If I don't cancel, I will receive 6 brand-new novels every month and be billed just $4.24 per book in the U.S. or $4.99 per book in Canada. That's a saving of 15% off the cover price! It's quite a bargain! Shipping and handling is just 50¢ per book.* I understand that accepting the 2 free books and gifts places me under no obligation to buy anything. I can always return a shipment and cancel at any time. Even if I never buy another book from Silhouette, the two free books and gifts are mine to keep forever.

235/335 SDN E5RG

Name _____ (PLEASE PRINT)

Address _____ Apt. #

City _____ State/Prov. _____ Zip/Postal Code

Signature (if under 18, a parent or guardian must sign)

Mail to the Silhouette Reader Service:
IN U.S.A.: P.O. Box 1867, Buffalo, NY 14240-1867
IN CANADA: P.O. Box 609, Fort Erie, Ontario L2A 5X3

Not valid for current subscribers to Silhouette Special Edition books.

Want to try two free books from another line?
Call 1-800-873-8635 or visit www.morefreebooks.com.

* Terms and prices subject to change without notice. Prices do not include applicable taxes. N.Y. residents add applicable sales tax. Canadian residents will be charged applicable provincial taxes and GST. Offer not valid in Quebec. This offer is limited to one order per household. All orders subject to approval. Credit or debit balances in a customer's account(s) may be offset by any other outstanding balance owed by or to the customer. Please allow 4 to 6 weeks for delivery. Offer available while quantities last.

Your Privacy: Silhouette is committed to protecting your privacy. Our Privacy Policy is available online at www.eHarlequin.com or upon request from the Reader Service. From time to time we make our lists of customers available to reputable third parties who may have a product or service of interest to you. If you would prefer we not share your name and address, please check here. ☐

Help us get it right—We strive for accurate, respectful and relevant communications. To clarify or modify your communication preferences, visit us at www.ReaderService.com/consumerschoice.

SSE10R

HARLEQUIN®

A *Romance*

FOR EVERY MOOD™

Spotlight on
— Heart & Home —

Heartwarming romances
where love can happen
right when you least expect it.

See the next page to enjoy a sneak peek
from Silhouette Special Edition®,
a Heart and Home series.

Introducing McFARLANE'S PERFECT BRIDE
by USA TODAY *bestselling author Christine Rimmer,*
from Silhouette Special Edition®.

Entranced. Captivated. Enchanted.

Connor sat across the table from Tori Jones and couldn't help thinking that those words exactly described what effect the small-town schoolteacher had on him. He might as well stop trying to tell himself he wasn't interested. He was powerfully drawn to her.

Clearly, he should have dated more when he was younger.

There had been a couple of other women since Jennifer had walked out on him. But he had never been entranced. Or captivated. Or enchanted.

Until now.

He wanted her—*her,* Tori Jones, in particular. Not just someone suitably attractive and well-bred, as Jennifer had been. Not just someone sophisticated, sexually exciting and discreet, which pretty much described the two women he'd dated after his marriage crashed and burned.

It came to him that he…he *liked* this woman. And that was new to him. He liked her quick wit, her wisdom and her big heart. He liked the passion in her voice when she talked about things she believed in.

He liked *her.* And suddenly it mattered all out of proportion that she might like him, too.

Was he losing it? He couldn't help but wonder. Was he cracking under the strain—of the soured economy, the McFarlane House setbacks, his divorce, the scary changes in his son? Of the changes he'd decided he needed to make in his life and himself?

Strangely, right then, on his first date with Tori Jones, he didn't care if he just might be going over the edge. He was having a great time—having *fun,* of all things—and he didn't want it to end.

Is Connor finally able to admit his feelings to Tori, and are they reciprocated?
Find out in MCFARLANE'S PERFECT BRIDE
by USA TODAY bestselling author Christine Rimmer.
Available July 2010,
only from Silhouette Special Edition®.

HARLEQUIN®

Super Romance®

Top author

Janice Kay Johnson

*brings readers a heartwarming
small-town story*

with

CHARLOTTE'S HOMECOMING

After their father is badly injured on the farm,
Faith Russell calls her estranged twin sister,
Charlotte, to return to the small rural town she
escaped so many years ago. When Charlotte
falls for Gray Van Dusen, the handsome town
mayor, her feelings of home begin to change.
As the relationship grows, will Charlotte
finally realize that there is no better place
than *home?*

*Available in July
wherever books are sold.*

HSR71644

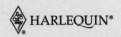